LIGHT EM UP

JONATHAN YANEZ
JUSTIN SLOAN

Jonathan Yanez

To my father and all the unsung heroes who served with him in the 82nd Airborne's Cougar Platoon during the Vietnam War.

Justin Sloan

To my fellow Marines, who helped to inspire my writing of these type of stories, and to all the fans of the Seppukarian Universe. It's because of you we are able to follow our dreams!

LIGHT EM UP TEAM

BETA AND JIT

Kelly O'Donnel

Alex Wilson

Leo Roars

Jackie Weaver

Becky Young

Tanya Wheeler

Rosemary Kenny

Holly Lenz

If I missed anyone, please let me know!

Editors

Kimberly Grenfell

Diane Newton

Kyle Noe

George S. Mahaffey, Jr.

Light Em Up (this book) is a work of fiction.

All of the characters, organizations, and events portrayed in this novel are either products of the author's imagination or are used fictitiously. Sometimes both.

"You need help. I don't just mean one psychiatrist. I mean, like, a full panel of multiple doctors working with you around the clock," Riot said, as she shook her head, taking in Vet's latest work of art. "And medication. Lots of medication. We're talking anti-psychotics, tranquilizers—the works."

"She looks good, right?" Vet ignored Riot's latest barrage. He crossed his arms over his chest. A deep sigh escaped his lungs. "I've been working on her day and night, but I think she's done."

Riot and Vet stood in the *Valkyrie's* engine room. In the rear of the hall-like chamber, past the quiet engine that powered the ship, the pair stood, inspecting Vet's project: a robotic body for the ship's AI, Evonne.

Since landing on Ketrick's planet of Hoydren a week before, they had received permission from

General Armon to go ahead with the plan. Vet had been hard at work, finishing the human-like body for Evonne, ever since.

What stood in front of them disturbed Riot to her core, mostly because the robot looked like a human being in every way. Everything from her long, silver hair, to her strong jawline and open, unblinking eyes screamed a human heritage. She wore a uniform like the rest of the crew, her mostly gray top and pants outlined with a white trim.

"I didn't do it all myself," Vet said, tapping the pointer finger of his right hand on his chin. "Doctor Miller helped a lot with … with the … with her anatomy."

"Riiiiiight." Riot let the word drag on.

"You do not approve of my physical body, Riot?" Evonne's ethereal voice sounded from the ship. The Australian accent Vet had chosen for her rang in her speaking pattern. "Should I not inhabit the physical form Corporal Vetash and Doctor Miller have prepared for me?"

"No, no," Riot said, shaking her head as she looked once more into the open grey eyes of the robot in front of her. "We received the okay from SPEAR, and you've been asking for this for a while now. You just gotta promise me you're not going to try to start an insurrection where machines wipe out humanity and the rest of the universe."

"I am incapable of such things," Evonne said

without emotion in her voice. "The only reason I have been requesting a physical body is to be of greater assistance to you and the crew aboard the ship. I will also do my best to blink around you. Perhaps minor human details such as these will put your mind at ease."

"All right," Riot said, and shrugged toward Vet. "How much longer until we put Evonne into the body?"

"I still have a few last minute updates to make." Vet pursed his lips and squinted at the robot's hands. His one eye studied the robot. The other eye he had lost in combat, and the area was fitted with a metal plate that looked like a patch. "I think I made her hands too big."

"Hey, whatever makes you happy," Riot shook her head, backing away. "I have enough issues to deal with without seeing my XO reshaping female hands."

"It's not as weird as you make it sound," Vet called to her back as Riot walked out of the engine room. "We're traveling through space and building alliances with aliens. Reshaping hands isn't that weird."

"Keep telling yourself that," Riot said, half laughing to herself.

Once Riot and her crew had departed from Admiral Tricon's Grovothe ship, it was decided they would travel to Ketrick's homeworld of Hoydren to support their off-world interests. It was Riot's and General Armon's beliefs that this planet once again would be the target of a Karnayer assault.

Not only was Hoydren the location of Earth's allies,

but the Karnayer, Remus, was also being held prisoner there. In addition to this, the Karnayers coveted the dragons that roamed the Hoydren skies and space. They wanted to capture and control them, eventually manipulating them to be used as their living weapons.

The Karnayer House led by Alveric was responsible for all the grief that had come Riot's way thus far. The captured Karnayer, Remus, was Alveric's brother, and Riot would bet her shorts that he was going to come to free his brother.

Upon landing, Riot and her crew had linked up with a newly promoted Colonel Harlan and his unit of scientists who acted as emissaries to the planet.

Riot walked through the halls of her ship, going through a checklist of things that needed to be done to fortify their position. If Alveric did attack with his Karnayers, Riot and the others would have to hold them off for the space of a few hours before General Armon could send aid from Earth.

As Riot walked down toward the rear cargo bay, she caught some banter passing between Rippa and Ketrick. The Grovothe major and the Trilord prince had been at one another's throats the entire trip, though their conversations were mostly playful jabs ... or at least that was what Riot kept telling herself.

"You remind me of a creature that roams the woods of my home planet. It's called a Sasquan," Rippa said to Ketrick as she worked on her mech unit in the cargo bay. "It's a smelly ogre of a creature with large feet and an ape-like face. Its intelligence factor is barely on the scale. Some would call it an idiot of a beast."

"Is that so?" Ketrick said. He stood on the opposite side of the cargo bay, scratching the underside of his dragon, Vikta's, scaly stomach. "If you were born here on Hoydren, your stunted body would have been sent to live outside the city out of the fear you would frighten the children. We would then tell stories of you to our young, stories that would threaten them, that if they behaved badly, you could come for them in the night and eat their faces."

"Hmmm..." Rippa nodded along with Ketrick's words as if she expected as much. She didn't move from her spot where she worked. "If you were born on my planet, we would call you a monstrosity and send you to work in the coal mines. Your dim wit and gargantuan body would make a great asset to the workers there. And, as a bonus, they wouldn't have to lay eyes on you. It's dark in the obsidian mines."

"It wasn't that funny," Ketrick growled at Vikta as the dragon cracked a toothy smile.

Vikta was in her smallest form now, no larger than a horse. It still amazed Riot that the creature was able to shift from something this size to her true form, a white dragon as large as her cruiser class ship.

Riot stood in the entrance to the cargo bay for a moment, admiring Rippa's twenty-foot armored mech and Ketrick's white dragon. How outrageous had her life become to now be able to make a trip to the cargo hold and see these wonders on a daily basis?

With a rueful smile, Ketrick raised one of his dark eyebrows in Rippa's direction. The long canine teeth that set him apart as a Trilord showed through.

"We have a name for your kind on our planet, as well, Major Rippa Gunna," Ketrick said, patting Vikta on her belly. "We call your kind dwarves."

Rippa dropped the tools she was working with at the feet of her mech unit. They slammed against the floor with a metallic ring. She stood and turned to Ketrick with a stare that could melt ice. For a moment, her fiery red hair seemed to be alive with the flames of anger.

"What did you call me?" Rippa clenched her hands on either side of her stout body.

"Hey, so the universe is going to hell in a handbasket, courtesy of Vet and Doctor Miller." Riot stepped into the cargo bay to diffuse the situation. "They're creating robots that can talk and think and pretty much run things. Insane, right? I mean, has no one ever seen those old Terminator movies, like, ever?"

Rippa remained silent, glaring at Ketrick.

The tall Trilord stood up from his kneeling spot beside Vikta. He ignored the death stares from the Grovothe and addressed Riot. "Interesting. I, for one, would welcome such an addition to the crew."

"Why's that?" Riot asked.

"I think it will be helpful to have an extra set of

hands aboard the ship," Ketrick said, nodding along with his own words. "More help to manage weapons inventory, man the bridge, and gather coffee."

"Coffee?" Riot rolled her eyes. Ever since Ketrick had discovered coffee aboard the *Valkyrie*, he had been obsessed. "Evonne isn't going to be your personal coffee assistant when she's up and running."

"Oh, of course not, of course not," Ketrick said, voicing the words while his red eyes twinkled with a mischievous grin.

Riot took a deep breath and shook her head. She hid the smile that begged to touch her lips at the Trilord's remark. "All right, Ketrick, with me. We need to assess the defenses again before tonight's meeting. There's a Karnayer prisoner I've been meaning to sit down and chat with, as well."

"Understood," Ketrick said.

Rippa finally released her anger and went back to maintaining her mech armor suit. Riot thought she heard the Grovothe mumbling under her breath something like "freaking giant," although she didn't actually use the word "freaking."

Riot strode onto the ramp that lowered out of the *Valkyrie's* rear bay. The ship's four thrusters set above the ramp created a kind of shade for a brief moment against Hoydren's twin suns.

The planet of Hoydren was both beautiful and brutal at the same time. With two suns in the sky, one white and the other orange, Riot could understand why most of the Trilord men walked around bare-chested, while the women wore short skirts and tops that looked like sports bras.

Riot felt another wave of heat hit her. Not for the first time her mind wandered to the idea of removing her own long-sleeved uniform and long pants for something more comfortable. As soon as the idea entered her mind, though, she pushed it out. She was a Marine, and certain things couldn't be changed. This was her uniform. She was a soldier, and soldiers didn't feel discomfort from something as trivial as the heat.

Riot and Ketrick walked past the *Valkyrie* and the other cruiser class ship, the *Titan*, that had transported Colonel Harlan and his team from Earth to Hoydren. Both crafts were docked within the capital city's walls. The city was built around a tall hill that overlooked the surrounding landscape in every direction.

The twin crafts sat next to the city's palace. Each level of the structure was shaped like a square. Every level that rose on top of another was smaller, giving the building a pyramid-shaped look.

Behind them and down the hill, the city was primarily made up of homes, while in front of the hill, sloping down toward the gates, businesses and markets rose on well-kept dirt roads.

"You've been worried these last few days, Sorceress," Ketrick said, using his nickname for Riot. "You are not yourself."

"What makes you say that?" Riot looked up at

Ketrick. She did her best to not allow her eyes to linger around his bare chest covered in tattoos.

"Because we've patrolled the city's defenses every day since we've arrived," Ketrick answered. He pointed down to the dense jungle on their right and the open plains on their left. "Don't think I'm not grateful for our walks, but we've been over this. When the Karnayers come, they'll hit us from the sky first. They'll unload their soldiers in the jungle to give them as much cover as possible."

"It's just something ingrained in me, I guess." Riot shrugged as the two stopped by the side of the palace. She studied the landscape for the hundredth time. "I plan and I plan some more, and then I do it over again. Despite the fact that nothing ever goes to plan."

"Despite that fact," Ketrick said, leaning against the side of the palace walls that rose up so tall, Rippa's mech would be able to fit underneath. "I believe as you do. The Karnayers will come. When they do, we'll be waiting. We'll defeat them."

"Not all of us share your unrelenting faith," Riot said, joining Ketrick to lean against the palace's hard exterior, placing a hand on the wall to either side of her. "Some of us, like yours truly, need to obsess about things."

"Leaders often do," Ketrick said, placing his hand on her own. "We never did get to go on that date."

Riot didn't move her hand away. If anything, she wanted to get closer to Ketrick, but now wasn't the time or the place. "We'll have nothing but time once the Karnayer threat is dealt with."

"You're not worried about what your superiors will say any more?" Ketrick asked.

"Like you said, you're not a Marine." Riot edged a bit closer to Ketrick so their arms touched. "I can't see them denying the request of the prince of Hoydren, the man next in line to rule over this planet."

Ketrick's red eyes lit with a mischievous light. "You know, we don't have to wait. We could always—"

Panicked shouts shattered the moment. Running feet sounded from around the palace.

"Story of my freaking life," Riot said, reluctantly removing her hand from Ketrick's.

2

Killa, the queen's general, rounded the corner of the palace, barking orders to her Trilords as she ran. "Find Riot at once. Lock down the city. Send out an alert to the city militia. I want everyone to know what happened."

Immediately, Trilord soldiers ran to do their leader's bidding. Killa looked up to see Riot and Ketrick as soon as she had relayed her orders.

"Trouble?" Riot asked, already knowing the answer.

"Always." Killa narrowed her eyes and looked from Ketrick to Riot and back again. "What were you two—"

"If it's a matter of importance, you should let us know immediately," Ketrick interrupted her. "We may be able to help."

"Of course." Killa motioned past her shoulder to the city below. "As you know, Remus had offered to trade secrets for a reduction in his sentence. He was playing us the entire time. As he was being moved to a different location from the hole we'd thrown him in, he escaped."

Riot felt her stomach do a backflip. She knew from the beginning that Remus' offer to cooperate had some ulterior motive, and here it was. He was just biding his time until he made his attempt.

"Clear the ships." Riot looked to Killa and Ketrick. "Lock the *Titan* and I'll leave the *Valkyrie's* rear cargo door open. They're the only ways off-planet. Remus will be forced to try to steal one if he's serious about leaving."

"Understood," Killa said, nodding slowly. "I'll send word to the crews immediately."

"I can stay with you," Ketrick said. His voice told Riot he already knew his words were uttered in vain.

"I'm a big Marine," Riot said, shaking her head. "Besides, if he sees anyone around, it'll spook him. I've got this covered. Don't worry yourself, Muscles."

Ketrick nodded slowly as Killa and her contingent of guards left to fulfill Riot's request.

"I'll be far enough away so to remain in the shadows, but I'll be there if you need me," Ketrick said.

"Agreed," Riot said, winking at Ketrick. "Ease up. I took down a Zenoth hive queen with a hammer, remember? I can take down one unsuspecting Karnayer."

* * *

Riot sat hunched behind Rippa's armored mech unit, her back pressed to the cold steel of the *Valkyrie's* hull. Why she had chosen this spot instead of a more comfortable one eluded her now. The area outside the ships had been cleared but for the normal Trilord patrol that would pass by every fifteen minutes. They couldn't make it too easy for Remus, or else he would expect the trap.

Maybe he suspected the trap already. He still had to come if he wanted to escape the Trilord city. The only other option would be to try to escape outside of the city walls. That would be the last thing Remus would want to do. There was no way off-planet for him in that direction.

Riot stretched her back to the limited extent that her small quarters provided. She could see the dying light outside of the open cargo bay doors. The twin suns that warmed the planet of Hoydren were making their final descent as the planet's giant moon took over its reign of the sky.

Whose brilliant idea was this again? Riot asked herself as she did her best to relieve her cramped aching muscles. *Oh yeah, you did this one to yourself. Good job, Riot. Now your muscles are cramping, it's hot, and you skipped dinner.*

Riot's mind was beginning to wander. Had it been an hour, or three? She was starting to lose focus when a shadow crossed the cargo bay door. In a second, her senses heightened. A rush of adrenaline sent her heart beating faster.

She peeked around the edge of the mech unit's giant leg. Remus stood in the entry way of the cargo bay doors. He looked nothing like she remembered. The once-proud Karnayer leader was a poor imitation of his former self. His white hair was filthy and matted. His blue skin was bruised around his eyes and mouth. The black clothing he once wore was gone, and instead, he wore pants and a tattered, white long-sleeved shirt.

Whatever the Trilords had done to him to exact their vengeance had been brutal. Riot felt pity for him, but for only a second. Remembering the lives he had taken, the dragons he had so cruelly enslaved and bent to his will, wiped away any of the sprouting pity she held in her chest.

Remus crested the cargo bay ramp. He hugged the opposite side of the ship, trying to make himself as small as possible.

Riot sprang from her place behind the mech unit. She raced across the cargo bay hold and threw herself at a wide-eyed Remus. The two went down in a pile. Remus clawed at her, trying to find a dominant position on top. He was taller and lankier than Riot, but she had the edge in muscle.

Riot fought past his arms and slammed him onto his back. The Karnayer's head bounced off the steel floor and he lay stunned for a moment. Riot took the opportunity to drag him to his feet and throw him against the cargo bay wall as hard as she could. His nose broke against the metal wall as he slumped to the ground. Blue blood raced down his nostrils while a wild look crossed his eyes.

"This can be as painful as you want to make it," Riot said, readying herself for another onslaught from the Karnayer. "You're beaten. Give up. Or don't, and I'll put you down again. I don't care."

Remus snarled and lunged at her once more.

Riot sidestepped his attack. Letting her guard down was a bad idea. He swung with a wild backhand and hit her in the mouth. Pain exploded across her jaw. The familiar taste of blood touched her lips.

"Oh, hell no," Riot said. She arched back her right leg and caught Remus in the torso with every ounce of strength she could muster.

Ribs cracked inside the Karnayer's chest as her boot made contact. He doubled over, falling to the ground.

"Want to go again?" Riot asked, spitting blood from her mouth. The nanites that healed her wounds were already at work. Riot ran her tongue over the place where her lip had been split. It was strange to feel the wound already closing. "I don't want to commit a hate crime, here, but if you come at me again, I'm going to beat you like you stole something."

Remus glared up at her again. For a moment, she thought he would try another assault, but she mistook defiance for defeat. Instead of trying to regain his feet, Remus stayed on the ground, clutching his chest.

"You think you've won?" Remus snarled. "My brother will come for me, and with him, the full force of the House of Karn. I'm not going to give you or your kind anything."

"Yeah, I didn't think so," Riot said. Out of the corner of her eye, she saw Ketrick at the base of the cargo bay ramp, along with a unit of Trilord soldiers. They waited there for her signal. "When I heard you offered to cooperate I didn't believe it. Now I know it was only so you could try to escape."

"Your superiors were too eager to try to make a deal for the knowledge I possess." Remus looked to his left to take in the group of Trilords at the cargo bay entrance. "I've given them nothing. There is no form of torture I won't endure. The Trilords have starved and beaten me, to no avail."

"Interesting." Riot pursed her lips. "Evonne, are you there?"

"I am," Evonne, the ship's AI, said from nowhere and everywhere at once. "What can I assist you with this evening?"

"Can you get Wang in here?" Riot said as a plan formed in her head. "I want to try something."

"Immediately," Evonne answered.

Remus eyed Riot with a suspicious glare.

"Come on in, guys." Riot waved over to the group of

Trilords gathered at the cargo bay exit. "You can all be part of this, too."

Ketrick, Killa, and two other hefty Trilords walked in. Their weapons were lowered at Remus.

"Are you injured?" Ketrick asked.

"What? This?" Riot pointed to her lip. "Already healed."

Wang came at a sprint from around the corner of the ship. He was out of breath but looked to Riot for direction. "I was ... I left the *Valkyrie* like you ordered."

Riot grinned at one of her oldest friends. Wang's short Mohawk-styled hair, his sharp features, and his athletic frame were nothing compared to his intellect. He was the smartest soldier she had ever come across and she was proud to call him her friend. Not that she would ever admit any of that.

"You're good. I told you to leave," Riot reassured him. "I was just wondering if you could cook up a truth serum cocktail for our friend, here. It doesn't seem like he wants to cooperate."

Wang looked over to Remus with a wide smile. "I think I have just the thing. I've been experimenting with concentrated dosages of sodium thiopental and the purest form of Scopolamine. What I've found is that, when introduced to the patient's bloodstream, the effects have been—"

"Wang, Wang." Riot lifted a hand and shook her head. "No one here understands what you're saying. I get that you're super excited about it, but Ketrick's eyes are glazing over."

"No, I'm sure he understands," Wang said, looking to Ketrick for help.

"It's true, brother Wang." Ketrick shrugged. "You lost me as soon as you opened your mouth."

Wang shifted his gaze to Killa and the two other Trilords in attendance. The two Trilords next to Killa shrugged.

"I tried to follow along," Killa offered, "but it was no use."

"Wang? Uh, Wang...?" Riot said, reeling him back in. "Just go grab it."

"Right," Wang said, shifting from a defeated look back to his normal, jovial nature. He took off at a run through the cargo hold to the med bay.

"If you think injecting me with some kind of arcane liquid that is meant to make me speak the truth will work," Remus spat, "then you are more of an idiot than I took you for."

"You are just a miserable person, aren't you?" Riot said, shaking her head. "Do you have any friends at all? I mean, besides your brother."

"I am very popular on my planet," Remus said, glaring at Riot and the Trilords around him. "I have plenty of friends."

"Uh, I think he's telling falsehoods." Ketrick leaned on his weapon, a long staff with a hammerhead and an axe head on either side of a blaster. "No one would want to be his friend."

"This is childish!" Remus roared. "I'm not going to sit here and argue about my relationships on my home planet."

Wang sprinted back into the room, carrying a syringe.

Ketrick and Killa pointed their weapons at Remus as he shot them murderous stares. Still, he didn't move as Wang injected him on the right side of his blue neck with the serum.

"You fools are wasting your time." Remus wiped his bloody nose. "I will never give up my family's information. I will never…"

Remus's voice trailed off like he had forgotten what he was going to say next. A blank look came over his eyes.

"How fast is this stuff supposed to work?" Riot asked Wang.

"I don't know," Wang said as he shrugged. "It's the first time I've used—"

"Oh, you're right, you're right." Remus hunched his shoulders as his lower lip protruded. In a sad voice, he admitted, "I don't have any friends."

3

R iot couldn't believe what she was seeing or hearing. Remus looked like a little kid sitting on the cargo bay floor. There was a sadness in his eyes, and his tone said he was nothing but sincere as he continued.

"I push everyone away," Remus said with a shake of his head. "Even my brother who's coming to rescue me doesn't really care about me. He's just doing it to uphold the family name. When he gets here and I'm free, it will be a constant mocking point for him. I'm never going to live this down."

Riot exchanged looks with Wang, who shrugged. "I guess it's working."

"I just … I just wish there was another way," Remus said, continuing on. He lowered his eyes to the floor as hot tears streaked his face. "Not only have I failed my family, but now I'll also be labeled as a failure in life.

Captured by a group of primitive Trilords and humans who have only just discovered the ability to travel off their own planet. I'm a disgrace. A no-good, friendless disgrace."

"Hey, hey there, little guy," Wang said as he took a seat next to Remus on the ground. "You'll be all right. We've all made some pretty serious mistakes in life. I mean, there was this one time I ate some shady Mexican food from a street vendor in Tijuana. He had a kind face, so I thought he could be trusted. That food ruined me. I spent all night and most of the next day on the toilet, beating myself up. I mean, I knew better."

Ketrick was the only Trilord who knew Wang well enough to crack a smile. Killa and her two other guards looked at one another in confusion.

"I don't think Remus is going to pose a problem to us for a while," Riot said to the Trilords, who still had their weapons leveled at Remus. "Why don't you let us see what we can find out, and we'll bring him back to you."

Killa looked over at Ketrick for a consensus.

"I'll stay here," Ketrick assured Killa and her two soldiers. "We'll bring him back as soon as we find out whatever it is we can."

"Understood." Killa lowered her staff and motioned to the two Trilord soldiers to follow her from the ship. "We'll be waiting to receive him once you are through."

"Ugh," Remus exhaled, watching Killa and the two

other Trilords walk out of the cargo hold. "She's so mean. Why is she so mean?"

"I don't know," Wang said as he let a heavy breath of his own escape his lungs. "Some people are heartless."

"Wang, I don't mean to break up the bromance here, but we need to stay on point," Riot said, reeling her corporal back in. "Focus. We need to find out what he knows."

"Oh, right," Wang said, placing a hand on Remus' shoulder. "Remus, we need to know when your brother is going to come for you and where he's most likely to strike."

Remus nodded along, wiping hot tears from his eyes. "He's here already."

"What?" Ketrick said confused. "Where? On Hoydren? How do you know?"

"It's our way to recruit local militia to do our fighting for us and keep our own ranks strong," Remus explained. "He'll be doing what I would have done. He's meeting with the Brute faction of the Trilord race once more to get them to join his army and fight against you. He'll probably try to capture more of your dragons, as well."

"No way," Riot looked to Ketrick for conformation. "The Brute force wouldn't fall for the exact same trick again, would they? They were already duped and defeated once."

"I don't know." Ketrick rubbed a hand on the underside of his jaw. "I wouldn't have thought the

Brutes would have taken up the Karnayer banner the first time. Maybe we should pay them a visit."

"His next move, whether the Brutes agree or not, will be an orbital strike from his destroyer," Remus continued to relay information, unprompted. "After that, he'll harass you with Scarab ships, forcing you to keep your heads down while he sends transport ships to unload soldiers and whatever other abominations he has with him. His destroyer is called the *Devastation*, by the way."

"I'm going to need some coffee for this." Ketrick looked over to Riot and Wang. "Do either of you want a cup?"

"How many have you had today?" Riot raised an eyebrow as she looked over at the prince.

"Four or five mugs, I think," Ketrick said, looking up at the cargo bay ceiling as if his answer was written there somewhere. "I can't be sure."

"You have a serious problem." Riot waved Ketrick away with an open hand. "Go. Go get your fix."

Ketrick smiled as he left the cargo hold.

"Let's hope he doesn't ever figure out what espresso is." Wang shook his head with a shudder. "He'll start talking as much as Doc Miller."

Riot smirked, but refocused her attention on Remus. It seemed that he was being nothing but genuine; however, a number of questions still needed to be answered.

"What abominations will Alveric offload on

Hoydren?" Riot asked. "You're talking about weapons, right?"

"Yes." Remus nodded. "Like I said, the Karnayer way is to travel from planet to planet, either convincing the local species to join us or forcing them to do so when they refuse. We have done this for centuries and will continue to do so. Why use our own resources when we can send others to fight and die for us? Alveric will come with warriors from other planets—some monsters, some calculating creatures, but they have all bent their knee to The House of Karn, as will you."

Riot wasn't one to be shaken or intimidated. A life in the corps had taught her that she was the one to be feared. The thing that did give her pause was the sincerity in Remus's words; he honestly believed the Karnayers would prove victorious.

"Whoa, whoa … that's some heavy stuff." Wang shook his head and got back to his feet. "You've got some issues, man. I can't blame you, either. It sounds like you were born into it. A product of your environment."

Riot stood quiet, considering her options. She still had so many questions to ask Remus, in the forefront being who these Ancient Ones were that the Karnayers served, and how exactly their magic ability worked. Topics she was just still beginning to understand.

She was forced to deal with the most pressing matter at the moment, though. If Remus was telling the truth, then Alveric was already here with a small force, trying to convince the Brute faction of the Trilords to join him once again.

"He's not such a bad guy," Wang said, coming to stand next to Riot. "He's been brainwashed to believe these things his entire life."

"He still has to be held accountable for his actions," Riot said.

"What did I miss?" Ketrick walked back into the cargo bay, blowing on a steaming cup of black coffee. "Anything important?"

"We're going to go visit the Brutes," Riot said, crossing her arms over her chest. "If Remus is right, the Karnayers are already on Hoydren. The fight is already at our door. Ketrick, Wang, take Remus back to Killa and let her know what's going on. I'll get the others."

"Roger that," Wang said, looking over to Remus. He helped the still-bleeding Karnayer onto his feet. "Let's go, little guy."

Ketrick moved with them, one hand on his weapon, the other still holding his coffee.

"Evonne," Riot spoke to the AI living inside the ship.

"Yes, Riot?" Evonne answered back.

"It's time to assemble the War Wolves," Riot said, speaking the name for her crew. "Tell them to return to the ship as fast as possible. It's time to fight."

4

"Why didn't we just bring the Trilord army with us?" Doctor Miller sat in her seat on the bridge of the *Valkyrie* next to Wang and Rippa. "We could fit dozens of them on the ship."

"If Remus is wrong about this, then we'll have summoned the army to fight for no reason," Riot answered, looking over to her left from her command chair. "If there is a fight, we can handle it. We'll need every Trilord warrior ready and rested for the main Karnayer engagement when it comes."

Doctor Miller nodded along with Riot's words as she turned back to her control panel.

Two minutes until we arrive, Rizzo's message appeared on the main screen in red lettering for Riot to see.

"Roger that." Riot looked over to Ketrick, who sat on her right. "You're sure this is the best place to touch down?"

"It's far enough from the Brute capital where they can't see us, but not too far so that we won't be able to run there within the hour," Ketrick said, so fast it was like his sentence was made up of one word. He fidgeted in his seat. His red eyes were wide, and there was a playful smile on his face. "We should gear up before we leave the ship."

"Are you on drugs?" Vet said, studying the Trilord beside him with his own good eye. "Are you sweating?"

"My heart feels funny." Ketrick placed a hand over his massive chest. "Your coffee is wonderful."

Riot was about to give more instruction, when something out of the front window caught her eye. Hoydren's twin suns had set. A massive silver moon hung in the sky with hundreds, if not thousands, of stars twinkling far above. What caught her attention wasn't the forest canopy below or the fires of a city barely visible in the distance. It was the sight of roaring fires and billowing smoke that rose into the night sky. The smoke was difficult to see at first, but the fires were clear.

"Are those … are there buildings on fire?" Riot craned her neck forward. She answered her own question as her eyes confirmed the news. "Remus was right. The Karnayers have already landed on Hoydren."

"That's the Brute's capitol." Ketrick stood from his seat to get a better view. "The entire city's on fire!"

It was true. As Rizzo brought the ship closer, what had once seemed like a few lights or some small fires suddenly expanded in size. Entire buildings were aflame, and the devastation only grew the closer and closer they got to the city.

Soon, the bright blaster beams of green-and-yellow weapons fire could be seen below.

"Evonne," Riot said, having seen enough, "you have the helm. Set us down right in the middle of wherever the Karnayers are. Wolves, time to gear up—double time!"

A chorus of "Rogers" sounded over the bridge, as well as Evonne's own confirmation that she had received the orders.

Riot ran to the armory room with the others. The humans, including Doctor Miller, began stripping down to their underwear to apply their dragon skin layer of under armor, as well as the next layer of liquid armor that would go on over that.

Rippa's gear was stowed next to theirs; however, her uniform was a tight-fitting grey leotard that would make movement in her mech easier. The emblem of a black helmet on the chest area of her uniform designated her unit belonged to the Spartan mech class.

We need to replace that emblem on her uniform, Rizzo

signed to the others as he shrugged on his red liquid armor. He pointed to the fierce wolf sigil of their own unit emblazoned on the shoulder of their armor. *We gotta jump her into the pack.*

"Yeah, we should do some hazing." Vet grabbed his Longshot 1000 sniper rifle whose scope was just as long as its barrel. The flat, black weapon was long but lightweight. It fit perfectly in his hands. "Maybe make her get a tattoo like Wang did."

"Too soon," Wang said, glaring at his friends. "I thought we were all getting those tattoos together. You all lied to me."

"You were wasted and did that all by yourself." Riot grinned as she clipped two Boomballs onto her belt with her molten blade. Along with the warhammer on her back, the Cannon FP290 on her hip, and the Villain Pulse Rifle in her hands, she was armed to the teeth. "Remember how he kept asking us if we were going to howl with him after his tattoo was finished?"

"What an idiot," Rippa said with a smile on her face. She stood at the door of the armory ready to depart. "No offense."

"You can't just say whatever you want to say and then say 'no offense.'" Wang shook his head, joining Rippa by the door. "Words do hurt."

"You are like a man-child." Rippa rolled her eyes as she left the armory room. "I'll be firing up my mech in the cargo bay."

"Riot," Evonne's Australian accent sounded over the ship's comms. "We are about to touch down as requested. There are no Karnayer forces that I've seen, but there is a gathering of Brutes in the center of the town."

"Land there." Riot grabbed her helmet in her free hand and motioned for her unit to follow. "Let's move out."

Riot led her crew through the *Valkyrie's* halls to the cargo bay where Rippa had just entered her mech unit. The twenty-foot-tall robotic piece of machinery came to life as a dull blue light glowed from its helmet. The helmet was shaped like one found on an ancient warrior in a time long past.

Vikta was also in the cargo bay. The dragon could sense something was wrong. She was probably already communicating with Ketrick through the telepathic bond they shared.

The ship touched down a moment later, sending a brief shudder through the hull. Riot placed her helmet on her head. The familiar heads-up display soon showed her readouts of, not only the weapons she and her men carried, but also of the Trilord and Grovothe on her team.

"Evonne, lower the cargo bay ramp." Riot tried to sound as optimistic as possible as she continued to her team. "Stay frosty. We don't know where the Brute's alliances lie, or if we'll encounter any Karnayers or creatures they've brought with them. Eyes open. Rizzo, if you see anything suspicious, just shout."

This brought laughs from everyone except for Doctor Miller.

Hahaha, Too Soon, Rizzo typed on the control pad on the back of his left forearm's armor.

"We shouldn't tease about other people's disabilities," Doctor Miller said as she inhaled a breath of air.

"Take it easy HR, it was a joke." Riot lifted her weapon as the cargo bay ramp came down in front of them. "Wang, you're attached to Doctor Miller's hip. Don't let Cupcake out of your sight."

"Roger that," Wang responded.

As soon as the cargo bay's doors were low enough for Riot to fit through, she moved forward in a crouch. Her senses were on overdrive as she aimed down the barrel of her weapon, her head on a swivel.

Evonne had indeed landed them in the middle of the confrontation. Although there was no weapons fire being exchanged at the moment, it was clear they had missed by minutes whatever it was that had happened there.

The *Valkyrie* sat in what looked like a town square. A cracked fountain stood right in front of them, surrounded by charred grass. On every side of the fountain were buildings two to three stories tall made of hard brick and stone.

Riot's heads-up display read dozens of Trilord

signatures. The tech built into her armor outlined the heat signatures to such a degree, Riot could even see that the Trilord Brutes were hiding behind doors, crouched behind windows, even lying in back rooms.

"Ambush?" Vet said through the comms.

"Not an ambush," Ketrick responded. "They're hiding, terrified of something. Vikta can smell their fear from here."

Something that sounded like a whale's call erupted from their right. Riot held a fist in the air for her team to hold and crouch. The noise came again, reverberating through the night to their position. The only light in the area was from the many fires that had erupted across the town. The buildings in every direction were in various states of repair, and those that had escaped the fires had caved-in walls or roofs.

The noise came again, so deep now, Riot could feel it in her chest. She zeroed in on the sound's location—a building a block away, one that looked like a warehouse.

Great, so here we go again, Riot thought. *Alien planet, check. Weird alien monster, check. Riot, why don't you go see what's making all those horrific noises, check.*

"KETRICK, you know these people better than I do," Riot said, making a split-second decision. "You and Doctor Miller with me. Vet, you hold here next to the ship and don't take your eyes off that warehouse where the noise is coming from. I have a bad feeling about this."

"Roger," Vet said over the comms. He started doling out defensive positions to the rest of the unit as Riot made her way to the closest building.

To their left, a two-story building whose right wall had crumbled in on itself stood out against the smoke-filled sky. Riot's and Doctor Miller's helmets would filter out the smoke, but Ketrick, who strode next to them, was taking in the noxious fumes. Riot lowered her weapon as they closed in on the building. It was obvious the Trilords had been attacked. If they were hiding, then Riot had no reason to engage them.

"We're not your enemies!" Riot shouted into the building. "We've come to help you. What happened here?"

Riot's heads-up display that showed her the outlines of four hunched figures in the building beeped to life as it counted everything from their weapons to how fast their hearts were beating.

"Ketrick," Riot said, motioning with her head to the wooden door in front of them. "I know they're part of your people's rival faction, but they're Trilords, just like you. Maybe they'll speak with you instead of a total stranger."

Ketrick nodded his approval. A cough escaped his lips as he took a step forward, lowering his own weapon. They were fifty feet from the closest building now.

"Most of you know me, or at the very least have heard of me. My name is Ketrick Warbringer, Heir to the Savage throne, Judge to my people, and he who speaks with the space serpents." Ketrick took a breath. "If I wanted you dead, I would rend your heads from their bodies with my bare hands or call the space serpents down on you to extract their vengeance for what you have allowed to be done to them."

"Okay..." Riot looked over to Ketrick, shaking her head. "Not really what I had in mind when I asked you to speak with them."

"Trust me." Ketrick looked down at Riot with a wink. "This is how we communicate."

Riot was about to tell Ketrick she would take point on dealing with the Brutes, when motion on her heads-up display quieted her words. The Brutes inside the building were moving. Not yet ready to welcome the strangers, they peeked out through broken windows in the building.

Riot caught sight of their large frames and wild yellow eyes that glinted from the reflection of fires raging in the city. The long canine teeth that sprouted from their upper jaws fell past their lips. In any other case, a group of warriors such as these would have made Riot lift her weapon and fire. But something in their eyes, in their very faces, told her she had nothing to fear from them. They were terrified.

"You can come out." Riot slung her weapon over her shoulder and removed her helmet. "I'm taking off my helmet because I trust that we're on the same side against whatever it was that did this to your city. If you shoot me in the face, I'm going to be pissed. If you end up killing me, I swear I'll haunt you from the grave."

The brute Trilords in the building looked to someone deeper inside the house for direction. Riot picked up on whispers and broken pieces of the conversation.

"She was the one who arrived not weeks ago, during the battle with the Savages."

"Boris was misled."

"She's one of the humans? Maybe she can help."

More hushed whispers.

Finally, the door to the building opened, revealing a lean Trilord who looked like he was old enough to be Ketrick's father. A thick, grey beard fell down his chin. Long, braided hair had been gathered behind his head in a knot. He looked at Riot with sad, wary eyes. There was wisdom in his weathered, wrinkled face and, to Riot's surprise, no fear whatsoever.

"My name is Talon," he said, opening his hands on either side of his body to show them he carried no weapons. "If you are truly here to help us, then help us."

The deep, whale-like moan rumbled through the air once more. Riot chanced a quick look behind her. Past the line where Vet had set up the rest of the crew, the warehouse building glowed with a strange white light.

"What's making that noise?" Riot asked, tearing her eyes from the warehouse building. She directed her attention back to the aged Brute in front of her. "What happened here?"

"The devil came to visit." Talon stared over Riot's shoulder with emotionless eyes. "And death came with him."

5

R iot stood stunned for a moment, trying to process what Talon had just said. It was clear he believed the information he had just related to her; there was no joking tone in his voice, no twitch of his lips.

"The devil?" Doctor Miller repeated, clearing her throat like she had just choked on her own saliva. "The devil?"

Doctor Miller looked over to Riot for direction. "The devil?"

"Yes, yes, that's what the man said." Riot refused to acknowledge the fear in the doctor's voice. "Let's move on from that."

"Start from the beginning," Ketrick encouraged the Trilord. "Who came, what did they look like?"

"It was the Karnayers, like they had come before,"

Talon spoke in a firm voice, despite what he had just been through. "Our new leader refused to help them this time. We've learned our lesson well, Prince. Boris died in the assault against your home. We elected a leader who is focused on helping us grow outside of war with the Savage faction. When we told the Karnayer as much and refused to help him, he unleashed the devil on our city."

"And what does this devil look like?" Riot asked.

"As tall as a building, with horns that protrude from its head. And ... and the ability to raise our dead and make them fight against us." Talon had said this last part as if getting the words from his mouth was harder than he'd anticipated. "I've seen them. I've seen our warriors killed and then brought back like dead, mindless creatures willing to obey the orders of our enemies. They've only attacked our capital city now, but if we allow them, it will spread.

"Help us? Will you help us?" A Trilord woman, seeing that Riot and her unit were willing to give them aid, ran from the supposed safety of a dark house. She grabbed Riot by both shoulders, trembling. "Please, you don't understand what we've seen here. It's ... it's impossible, what's going on."

"Get ahold of yourself, woman." Riot freed herself from the much larger Trilord's grip. It took all she had not to level the Brute when she had rushed her. The one thing that had stilled her hand, though, was the look of pure dread in the woman's yellow eyes. "We are going to help. We just have to gather some information."

"Oh, thank you, thank you," the woman prattled on. "The Karnayers came from the sky. When our leader refused them, they unleashed the devil on us. It was something out of a nightmare!"

The woman grabbed Riot again, screaming about devils and demons from the abyss.

SMACK!

Riot had slapped her across the face, so hard, it made the Trilord woman's head turn. Riot was a Marine, not a saint. She didn't open hand slap people often, but when she did, she had a good reason for doing so. "Control yourself. You're making this situation worse right now. Let's focus on the solution now, not the problem."

The woman looked stunned, but nodded along with Riot's words.

More and more buildings in the town center opened their doors. Now that they saw Riot and her unit were indeed there to help, they were more willing to show themselves. These Trilords were mostly elderly men, women, and children.

It seemed those Trilords in the area capable of fighting had run off to defend the city.

"That's what was bothering me before," Ketrick said, placing his long weapon over his shoulder. "There are no bodies."

Riot took a moment to process his words. She

scanned the area, noting the same thing. Familiar signs of struggle when a firefight opened up in a populated area like this met her eyes: scorch marks from explosions, crumbling buildings, and fires in the area. Ketrick was right, however: no corpses on the ground, no wounded.

"Keep your people inside, and stay down," Riot told Talon and the woman in front of her. "We share a common enemy. We'll take care of this."

"Be careful," Talon warned. "Stay away from its breath. It brought them back with its breath."

Riot nodded. She turned and walked back to the rest of her unit stationed by the *Valkyrie*.

"What do you think that means?" Doctor Miller asked through her comm. "Stay away from its breath? It brings back the dead with its breath?"

"I don't know, but you'd best believe we're going to find out." Riot placed her helmet back on her head. "Even if it does have a bad case of morning breath, I've never met anything that can't be killed."

"I can bring Vikta along," Ketrick said, thinking of the crew's largest member. "She'll be more than a match for anything inside that warehouse."

The noise came again. The low, deep sound of moaning, if moaning was done in a singsong wail, and it was unlike anything Riot had ever heard. Goosebumps raced down her arms, and a chill touched her spine like a cold finger racing down her back.

"We'll keep Vikta in reserve until we find out exactly what's going on," Riot told Ketrick. "The last thing we need is our dragon caught in a situation she can't get out of."

Ketrick nodded along with Riot's words.

"All right," Riot said, reaching the rest of her unit, who had taken up defensive positions around the ship and the broken fountain that rested in the middle of the town square. "It looks like the Karnayers have brought with them some kind of creature that raises the dead."

"You're joking, right?" Vet looked over from his crouched position behind a broken piece of stone. "Zombies? We're going to be fighting zombies?"

"Not zombies," Rippa's voice sounded over the comms from inside of her mech unit. Rizzo and Wang were stationed behind her. Rippa's mech unit's armor was so durable, it provided cover of its own. "A Devil's Hand."

"You know what this thing is?" Riot couldn't keep the shock out of her voice. "What's a Devil's Hand?"

"Nothing more than a story Grovothe tell their young to make them urinate before bedtime," Rippa answered, her voice distant as if she were willing some long-lost memory to the front of her mind. "Creatures from a planet I've only heard of in books. They lived somewhere near the universe's edge but were all thought to be extinct by now. They're large and have the ability to sing their dead victims into a state of servitude for them."

"Well, that would make sense," Riot said, thinking of what she had learned from Remus earlier that night. "The Karnayers must have captured one and now use it to do their will."

"Hold up. Are we just going to skip over the fact that this monster is so scary, Grovothe children piss their pants when they hear it?" Wang asked from his kneeling position behind Rippa's mech. "I'm not the only one who heard that, right?"

"I also heard the urinating story," Ketrick confirmed. "It is quite unnerving."

"Whatever," Rippa said. "It's the truth. We'll see how many of these undead you take under your blade compared to mine."

"Please, I will make my own enemies urinate themselves when they see me coming." Ketrick bristled. "I'll kill many more of them than you—"

"Okay," Riot said, lifting her voice over whatever Ketrick was about to say. "We're not doing this now. I want Vet and Doctor Miller on over-watch on the right side of the buildings. Vet, choose a spot and have the doctor watch your six."

"Roger that." Vet nodded, motioning for Doctor Miller to follow him.

"What? What am I supposed to do?" Doctor Miller looked from Riot to Vet. "That whole thing in the

Zenoth hive was a one-time deal. I don't know what came over me. I'm a non-combatant. I mean, I don't even like killing spiders!"

Vet must have switched their comm lines to a different channel because Doctor Miller's voice disappeared for the time being. Riot turned to the rest of her unit.

"All right. Ketrick and Vikta will be the cavalry. Once we check out what's going on in that warehouse, we'll signal them to flank the enemy. We need eyes on the target before that can happen. That means myself, Wang, Rizzo, and Rippa will take the left side of the road to the warehouse."

"We'll be ready," Ketrick said, starting to walk over to the *Valkyrie* where Vikta stood on all fours, her long snout sniffing the air. Ketrick looked over his shoulder a moment later. "Vikta says to be wary. Whatever is in that building is not of this world."

Thanks for the words of encouragement, Rizzo wrote over everyone's heads-up display. Ironically, Ketrick was the only one who wouldn't get the message, since he refused to wear a helmet.

"Let's go." Riot checked her Villain Pulse Rifle for the dozenth time. The Marines had turned her into a creature of habit, always checking and rechecking her weapons and equipment. "Rippa and myself in the lead; Wang and Rizzo bringing up the rear."

Riot vaulted over the waist-high debris they had

been using for cover. Rippa matched her quick stride with an easy gait of her own. Her mech was twenty feet tall, which meant taking slow strides to keep in formation with the others.

For the moment, Riot pushed everything out of her mind besides the pulsing white light that showed through the cracks of the doors and windows in the large warehouse building. In the interim, the wailing alien noises had subsided.

"Anything else you can tell us about this Devil's Hand?" Riot asked as she led her unit to the left side of the road. She hugged the buildings, welcoming any cover they could provide.

"I wish I could remember more," Rippa answered. "The stories were always horrifying. A monster from the depths of Hell, one that not only consumed your soul but brought your empty husk of a body back from the dead to serve it."

"All of a sudden I'm wishing I didn't ask," Riot said only half teasing.

The four members of Riot's team made their way down the road. Fifty yards from the building nothing had changed. There were no lookouts, no guards hiding to ambush them as they approached.

The stars overhead and the fires in the city were the only things that gave off light. Riot could switch to her night vision mode on her heads-up display, but there was no point. She would be made aware of any threat via the scanners in her helmet, and when they did get to the warehouse, the pulsing light coming from it promised enough illumination.

Twenty yards from the warehouse, Riot called a stop. There was an open road between them and the building. The pulsing light continued to glow off and on, but there was no noise. The entire city was as silent as a crypt.

"I vote sending Rippa to knock," Wang whispered in his comms. "She's got a tank built around her."

"Geez, thanks," Rippa muttered. "What a gentleman."

"I'm just saying," Wang said. "You're the best equipped for the present task."

"There's a window on the left side of the building about two stories up," Riot said as her heads-up display searched for access points to the large structure. "Rizzo and Wang hold here. Rippa, you'll give me a boost when we get there. Let's see what a Devil's Hand looks like."

Riot took off down the street, still sweeping to see if there were any hidden enemies lurking in the shadows. There were none. At the moment, Riot wasn't sure if that was a good thing or a bad thing.

Rippa followed quietly alongside. She took long strides, carefully placing her foot down onto the ground with every step. Despite her massive size, she was as quiet as Riot. Her armored mech moved like a human.

Riot reached the side of the warehouse in no time.

A better view of the building told her exactly what she had expected. It looked like a massive warehouse with a slanted roof. Two giant double doors were closed in the front, with a line of slender windows near the roof the only other access points.

"What's that?" Rippa asked as she crouched in her mech near Riot. She pointed with a massive hand to a wet spot pooling from the entrance to the warehouse.

Riot followed the fat, metal finger of Rippa's mech to the spot where she was pointing. Liquid was pouring out of the warehouse between the door and the ground. Riot zoomed in on the fluid, confirming her worst fears. It was blood.

"Let's just get this done." Riot bottled the fear she felt and reminded herself of the warrior she was. "The longer we wait out here, the more time we have to second-guess ourselves."

"I agree." Rippa lowered her mech farther to the ground, crouching so that Riot could climb onto her mech's left shoulder. "If fear was an option, I might be feeling it right about now."

"Good thing neither of us are the feeling type," Riot said. She slung her rifle across her back where her warhammer sat. Riot knelt on Rippa's mech unit's left shoulder. With her right hand, she held on to the mech's helmet, and with her left, she grabbed the mech's shoulder armor where the upper arm connected to the torso.

Rippa gently moved to a standing position, then

placed herself along the side of the warehouse. Riot's height standing on top of Rippa's mech was perfect. The window Riot looked through was grimy and streaked with smoke. She gently wiped away the coat of ash to see inside the warehouse. What her eyes found next was enough to chill her to the bone.

6

I f Riot let fear get in the way of doing what had to be done, then this would have been the time. Riot studied the inside of the room, sweeping her gaze back and forth. She knew what she was supposed to be doing—counting the enemies' number, searching for entrance points, gauging their weapons— but with what was going on inside the building, it was nearly impossible.

An army of bloodied Trilords stood shoulder to shoulder. Wounds ranging from severed arms to half of their faces missing told Riot these were warriors who were supposed to be long dead. Something very unnatural was keeping them alive.

And Riot could make an educated guess as to what that unnatural thing was. To the left of the window at the back of the building, a beast out of her nightmares stood on a raised platform. The closest thing Riot could relate the Devil's Hand to was a giant bull mixed with a crocodile. Horns sprouted from the monster's head, and it was covered in dark green scales, with a strong tail. It was roughly the size of a short bus. Its huge, bulky body made it clear it was not going to be taken down easily.

All of the zombified Trilords stood still, eyes looking at the creature as if they were somehow communing with the beast. Next to the monster stood a small group of Karnayers—six Karnayer soldiers dressed in black armor and carrying pulse weapons, and a seventh that Riot recognized.

Remus's brother, Alveric, stood with his hands clasped behind his back, grinning. His tall frame and the long, white hair that cascaded down his black robe familiar to his race was easy to pick out. Riot had only seen him once before while she talked to him over her ship's display screen, but she was positive it was him.

From out of nowhere, the Devil's Hand opened its giant maw, revealing rows of sharp teeth that reminded Riot of a shark's mouth. Out of its throat came the noise Riot had heard so many times already—the bass-like howling of a whale.

The Trilords in front of the beast had to number in the hundreds. They swayed from side to side as if the sounds somehow promised them peace.

Everything all right? Rizzo asked over Riot's heads-up display.

"Of all the words I could choose for this moment,

'all right' would be really far down the list. Like you showed up to the DMV without an appointment down the list," Riot said, realizing she was dealing with the moment by making light of the situation and not caring. "I'm going to link my heads-up display to everyone's so you can see what I'm seeing. Just expect the worse, and then double that. You'll be close."

Riot pressed a button on the control panel built into the backside of her left forearm. A light blinked off and on in the upper right hand corner of her screen designating, that everyone was now able to see what she was seeing.

"Holy mother of Moses," Doctor Miller inhaled. "Are they ... are they dead?"

"Never mind the army of zombies, look at the thing," Wang's voice reached everyone over the comms. "It looks like Godzilla got shrunken down to a miniature size and Cthulhu gave him horns."

"What's our move?" Rippa said with an unwavering tone. "I say we blow the entire warehouse to the next life and let the Allfather sort out the souls."

"I don't really disagree with you there," Riot said, considering her options. "All right, let's get back to the shi—"

"Can they see you?" Vet interrupted her in a very unlike-Vet way. "I think that one Karnayer over there is pointing at you."

"What?" Riot asked. "No they haven't seen—"

Riot looked over to the group of Karnayers

standing next to the Devil's Hand on the raised platform. One of the black-armored soldiers was definitely pointing in her direction with panicked motions of his right pointer finger.

"Oh, I think you might be right," Riot said, scratching the idea of blowing the whole warehouse to Kingdom Come and already forming plan B.

In the space of a heartbeat, every single head in the warehouse, Karnayer, zombie Trilord, and the Devil's Hand, all swung in her direction.

"Yep, yep, you're definitely right," Riot said, doing the only thing she could at the moment. She waved. "They see me, and I'm waving back to them right now."

At once, the silent, stunned trance everyone in the warehouse seemed to have erupted into an avalanche of chaos. The Devil's Hand bellowed. The army of Trilord undead woke from their stupor and ran for the building doors. The Karnayer force lifted their weapons and opened fire on Riot.

Riot ducked just in time as green blaster fire shattered the window around her, sending sharp shards of glass over her, and Rippa's mech below. Riot slammed the button on her heads-up display to remove the shared viewing option.

"Wang, Rizzo, Vet—you're weapons free on whatever comes out of the warehouse. Rippa, get us back to the rest of the unit. Ketrick, get ready to bring the cavalry."

Rippa turned her mech slowly enough for Riot to

keep her balance but fast enough to make her grab on for fear of falling off. With long, even strides, Rippa made the trip back to where the rest of the unit had taken up defensive positions in the cover of the building.

BOOM!

The warehouse doors exploded outward, releasing a horde of undead Trilords. Nearly all of them still had their weapons intact. Yellow fire from their hybrid staff and blunt force weapons showered the back of Rippa's mech. Riot dropped into a crouch. Despite her efforts to remain unscathed, a blaster round struck her in the back of her right shoulder.

Her armor held, but it felt like being hit with a baseball bat. A numb sensation raced across her right shoulder as she focused on not falling off of Rippa.

Rippa moved her mech into a tight alley right in front of where Rizzo and Wang pumped round after round into the coming zombie horde. Rippa knelt once more, allowing Riot to jump off.

"What's the good word, Wolves?" Riot shouted to be heard over the firing weapons. She swung her pulse rifle off her back and moved to peer around the building's corner.

"These zombies aren't going down," Wang shouted back. "I've hit a few, center mass, and they shrug it off like I'm shooting a marshmallow gun at them."

Riot took a knee and stuck her head and weapon around the corner. Wang was right. An ocean of

Trilords was less than a hundred yards from their location, and closing fast. When any one of them got hit with a round in the torso, they stumbled backwards for a moment, then continued on.

Riot aimed down her sights and tested a few rounds of her own on different body parts of the oncoming Trilords. She took one in the kneecap. The Trilord fell, but instead of writhing in pain, it continued to crawl forward.

She took one in the arm, with no result, and the final one in the head. The unlucky target was having one hell of a day. One second, the overweight, shaved-headed Trilord was lowering his blaster, which looked like a spear; the next, his head erupted in a shower of blood and gore. The body stumbled once, then remained still.

"Surprise, surprise, boys and girls," Riot shouted as she ducked back around the corner she used as cover. A hail of yellow blaster fire pinned her down for the time being. "The way to kill a Trilord zombie is the same way you kill any other. Plug them in the head. Oohrah! Let's light 'em up!"

The thumping sounds the Trilord weapons made were contrary to the loud booms of traditional fire the Marines used. It was a cacophony that covered the battlefield.

Then Rippa appeared around the corner.

VROOOOOM!

The Grovothe didn't waste any time unloading with

her most powerful weapon. A blue laser beam shot out of her mech's helmet. The beam cut through the oncoming Trilord horde like a group of kids at fat camp through an all-you-can-eat buffet. Trilords fell left and right as their heads were severed in two, bodies cut down the center, and limbs removed in an instant.

"Come on!" Rippa roared over the comms. "Fire everything you've got!"

No screams came from the victims, just the ever-present volley of return fire as the Trilord numbers began to thin. Riot and her Marines unloaded along with her. Vet, still in his over-watch position to the right, popped heads like balloons at a fair. Rizzo let loose with his Vulcan-like mini-gun that spewed red blaster rounds into the horde.

Things were just beginning to turn from nightmarish to just a bad dream, when the Devil's Hand charged through the open warehouse doors. The beast bellowed a war cry in its deep baritone voice. It sprinted at Rippa's mech with madness in its eyes.

"Bring it down!" Riot ordered, training her Villain Pulse Rifle at the beast, firing a concentrated burst at its head. "Rippa, watch out!"

To her unit's credit, they realized the threat the Devil's Hand held, and immediately opened fire on the charging beast. But Rizzo's Vulcan, and even Rippa's blue laser beam, failed to puncture the hide of the beast. If anything, they only infuriated it more.

Although the monster was only half as tall as Rippa's mech, it was twice as bulky. Its charging body looked like a heavy linebacker about to sack the opposing team's quarterback.

At the moment of impact, Rippa bent her mech's knees and threw her hands up. The monster dove at her, gripping her outstretched hands in its claws and, lunging forward with its short neck, it gripped Rippa's left shoulder in its teeth.

At once, the beast fell on top of Rippa's unit, and the next minute, its bulk bullied the power of her mech backwards to the ground.

"Ketrick," Riot yelled into her comms as she sent another round of blaster fire at the incoming Trilords closing the distance. "Now would be a good time!"

Right on cue, Ketrick descended from the heavens atop Vikta. The rider and dragon fell on the back of the massive, bull-like Devil's Hand. Vikta dug her claws deep into the creature's ribs. She grabbed the monster by the back of its neck in her jaws.

"I hope you remember that a stupid giant saved your life this day, dwarf," Ketrick laughed over the comms as he plunged the blade of his axe into the monster's hide. "I would never have fallen to such a simple brute."

"Yeah, how many enemies have you killed?" Rippa screamed back as she fought off the alien monster still on top of her. "I counted two dozen Trilord zombies I killed, while you were flying around in the sky like a little fairy."

"Pshhhh," Ketrick laughed. "Killing this creature makes for a hundred Trilord deaths."

"What—a hundred?" Rippa cried out in frustration. She battered closed fists at the head of the Devil's Hand's. "Who's making these rules?"

The conversation between Rippa and Ketrick took a back seat as Riot concentrated on the advancing Trilord throng. Rippa's laser beam had bought them time, but had not solved their problem. Still well over a hundred zombified Trilords were walking, crawling, and dragging their way forward.

For the first time, Riot caught sight of Alveric and his Karnayer guard at the rear of the fight. They stood in what they thought was the safety of the warehouse doors, looking on, while others fought and died.

If you can kill him now, this war can be over before it really begins, Riot thought. *It's not going to be easy getting to him, but then again, when has life ever been easy for you?*

"Vet, Wang, Rizzo, I'm going to need you to cut me a path to the Karnayers standing at the warehouse," Riot said, taking a deep breath and preparing herself for the run past the Devil's Hand and through the mass of zombified Trilords. "Try not to shoot me."

7

"Oohrah!" Vet yelled over his comms.

Get Some, Rizzo wrote over her heads-up display.

"When in Rome," Wang added with the others, like the saying belonged.

"I don't think that means what you think it means," Riot said as she licked her dry lips inside of her helmet. "Look that one up when we get back."

Without waiting for a response, Riot bolted from around the corner and made her run. She once more slung her weapon over her shoulder in favor of her two Boomballs that hung on her belt.

To her left, Ketrick and Vikta had managed to get the beefy Devil's hand off of Rippa. The creature's hide was so thick, not even Vikta's massive claws or razor-like teeth were able to puncture it.

But the Devil's Hand had more than met its match

in the Trilord and the Grovothe. Riot had to trust they would find a way to defeat the monster. She had more pressing things to deal with at the moment.

Riot ran in a crouch, doing her best to make herself a small target. She lobbed the grenade-like Boomballs into the ranks of the oncoming horde, then grabbed her rifle again and began making use of the target-rich environment.

Thump! Thump! Thump!

Yellow streaks of enemy energy blasts scorched the ground around her. The air cracked as numerous beams nearly struck her.

BAM! BAM!

Riot's Boomballs went off in quick succession, clearing her a path in the middle of the Trilord host. Riot's breath was heavy, her adrenaline adding to the spike in her heart rate.

A Trilord on her right raised a hammer-like weapon in her direction, and Riot took it out with a headshot. Aiming was nearly unnecessary; she was so close to the Trilords now, she was nearly on top of them. She fired again, opening up a hole the size of a grapefruit in her next victim's throat.

The smoke from her Boomballs washed over the ranks of the Trilords, making it difficult to see.

BOOM! BOOM! BOOM! BOOM!

Riot's Marines opened up all around her. Riot wasn't even fast enough to take down her own targets. Before she could line up a shot, their heads were already exploding, thanks to Vet's high-powered sniper rifle, or their bodies were turned to shredded cheese, courtesy of Rizzo's Vulcan-like mini-gun.

Riot was in the middle of the throng before she gave herself time to consider how insane her plan actually was. Trilords were firing so close to one another now, every shot that missed her took out one of their own.

Pain danced around Riot's left side as a blaster round found its mark. At this close range, it tore through her armor, scorching the skin underneath. Riot fought back a scream as the pain almost instantly subsided, the nanites in her body already rushing to the wound and healing tissue and skin.

Riot rolled under a club swing from her right and came back up, running. All around her, bodies were falling and heads were exploding as Vet and Wang opened up a route through the lines. Rizzo did the clean-up work as red blaster fire tore through the Trilord ranks.

Riot had given up firing on the mass, and just ran. A Trilord arm reached out and grabbed her weapon. Instead of coming to a standstill in the middle of swirling arms and weapons, Riot let go of her pulse rifle.

Another wave of pain exploded in her head as an axe landed against the right side of her helmet. Despite the helmet's protection, Riot saw stars. She stumbled for a moment, nearly falling to all fours.

Keep going, keep going, you got this! Riot screamed to herself. She fell to the ground a moment later as another round of blaster fire caught her in the foot. Riot ignored the pain. *Get back up, get back up!*

"Rawwww!" Riot forced herself to her feet again and half-ran, half-limped through the last lines of the Trilord army.

In front of her, Alveric stood twenty yards away behind his six bodyguards. The soldiers all leveled their weapons at her, black-painted rifles that looked capable of chewing holes through concrete.

Alveric began to clap. "Bravo. You made it through the lines of the dead. What now, Marine Riot? What did you think you would achieve by reaching me? What did you think you would achieve from fighting this battle at all? The Trilords are an insignificant race of meat shields."

"Sorry, sorry, you have something right … here." Riot pointed her right pointer finger to the outside of her helmet where the corner of her right lip would be. "I'm not kidding. I'm trying to pay attention to you, but it's just so hard. Did you … did you have ketchup or something with your dinner?"

"What are you talking about?" Alveric gave her a deep scowl. "I'm about to kill you, and you make your last words in this life a jest?"

"Just, just here." Riot wiped at her helmet again. "Just a dab, and we can get on with this. It's so distracting."

Alveric ran a tongue along the side of his face where Riot was pointing, then he brought up his right hand to smear away anything that might have been there. As soon as his eyes shifted down to look at his hand to see if Riot was telling the truth, she made her move.

Riot went into a crouch, while at the same time, bringing forward the warhammer on her back. She only had one chance at this; her aim had to be perfect. Riot stilled her beating heart as she aimed for Alveric's head.

Ignoring the six rifles that bore down on her was one of the hardest things she had to do, but if she wanted a chance of taking out Alveric, then this was it. Blaster fire erupted from both sides at the same time. The last thing Riot saw was the surprise on Alveric's face before pain erupted across her body. She managed to get off her own shot while she was being stricken by the green beams of energy.

Riot was struck in her left shoulder, abdomen, and right thigh. She rolled across the hard-packed dirt, praying her initial blast had hit her target, and opened up on the six soldiers in front of her.

THUMP! THUMP! THUMP!

The warhammer that was the favored weapon of the Trilords had two firing options, controlled bursts and full auto. The only danger of using full auto was the weapon overheated in the space of a few seconds. But a few seconds were all Riot needed.

Green fire peppered the area around her while Riot

hosed the soldiers in front of her with the returning yellow fire. While she focused past the pain and took out soldier after soldier, she got a better view of what had happened to Alveric. The Karnayer leader had been wounded, but not killed.

Riot's initial shot had been fired while she had been hit herself and the force of the impacts striking her own body had been enough to turn her aim ever so slightly. Instead of her round striking Alveric in the head, it had grazed his right cheek. In a bit of irony, blood now dripped from the wound on his mouth where a minute before Riot had convinced him he'd actually had something.

Riot took down one of the Karnayer soldiers with a burst to his stomach, and the next with a volley of fire to his helmet. Alveric was screaming obscenities Riot didn't understand, but she was pretty sure it had something to do with her mother.

Two of the four remaining Karnayer soldiers hurried Alveric back through the warehouse. The other two did their best to keep Riot pinned down.

Riot absorbed another blaster round to her torso before mowing down the last two remaining guards. Her overheated weapon felt like fire in her hands. The warhammer clicked dry a second later, refusing to send any other projectiles from its head until it rested.

Forcing her battered body forward, Riot held onto the warhammer and gave chase. Being wounded and instantly repaired by the nanites coursing through her body was a strange thing. She felt all of the pain for a brief moment when the enemy fire had hit her, but then, within seconds, the pain was already subsiding. Her body was healed in under a minute, and she was ready to go again.

Riot vaulted over the four dead Karnayer guards as she entered the warehouse. She screamed the name of her enemy, who fled in fear. "Alveric!"

Three figures sprinting through the warehouse were already halfway across the large building when the last two Karnayer soldiers turned at her words and opened fire.

At this range, Riot's warhammer was ineffective. Already overheated, it wouldn't be dispatching any enemies unless she was up close and personal, so Riot dropped the hammer. Her right hand reached for the Cannon FP290 at her hip.

The Karnayers fired wildly as she approached. Something about striking your enemy repeatedly and not seeing her fazed wore on the enemies' resolve to fight. They understood Riot wasn't going to die, and they were panicked. Riot almost felt sorry for them. Almost.

"Alveric!" she screamed again, her words echoing off the walls of the open room. She walked forward, her right arm extended with her weapon. Two well-placed shots ended the lives of the Karnayers in front of her. "Alveric! You can run, but I'm coming for you!"

Alveric disappeared though a side door at the rear

of the building. Riot turned her walk into a run and crossed the warehouse floor in minutes. She exited the back door in time to see a Karnayer transport ship roughly the size of the *Valkyrie* powering up. The ship had been hidden behind the warehouse building.

Riot opened fire on the craft, already knowing that her small-arms fire would do no lasting damage, yet refusing to stand there and do nothing. Her cannon was great at shredding body armor, but the hull of a ship was another matter.

The ship fired its thruster and lifted off the ground. A moment later, it was gone.

Riot gritted her teeth. She was so close to finishing this war, here and now. The fight to come would be bloody. Alveric wasn't exactly the forgive-and-forget type.

"Riot! Riot, are you okay?" Wang's voice came over the comms. "We're whipping up the last of the Trilords now. Do you need backup?"

"Negative," Riot said, turning back toward the warehouse. "I'm coming back to you. What's the status on the Devil's Hand?"

"His hide is too thick," Ketrick grunted over his comms like he was being bucked off a horse. "We can't get a killshot in."

Riot forced fatigued legs into a run as she crossed the warehouse again, and got a look at what was going on when she exited the building. The street was covered with the bodies of the Trilord zombies. A few here and there that had not been taken out by headshots still crawled around.

Riot ran back for her warhammer, then returned to wade through the knee-high battlefield of bodies, firing into the craniums of those who still pulsed with undead life. Her main attention was on the struggle still taking place between Ketrick, Rippa, and the Devil's Hand.

Vikta had the monster's head pinned down, with her mouth wrapped around its neck. The alien creature was on its side, still struggling to get back on its feet. The dragon's large frame was enough to keep it from being able to get back up, but only barely. Vikta flapped her wings as she readjusted her stance over her assailant. Ketrick brought the axe end of his spear down over and over again on the creature, to no avail.

Rippa did her part in her mech by controlling the back two legs of the creature's struggling feet.

"They've got it down," Wang said, as he and Rizzo appeared by Riot's side. "But there's no way to get through its skin."

The Devil's Hand twisted its head, trying to line its mouth toward Vikta. It opened its maw and sent a white, pulsating light from deep within its throat. The same whale-like echo shattered the air in an eerie song.

"Don't let Vikta get hit by the Devil Hand's breath," Rippa shouted over the comms. "I don't know what it will do to her."

Riot looked on, helpless. It was too late.

8

The pulsating and unnerving white luminescent light came from the creature's mouth and caught Vikta in the face. The dragon reared back, stunned for a moment.

The Devil's Hand took advantage of the distraction. Getting its front two feet underneath its massive bulk, it flipped its tail, sending Rippa's mech flying through the air and crashing into a two-story building behind her. The mech disappeared behind crashing walls and a crumbling roof.

"Fire everything you've got!" Riot went down to one knee, aiming her now cooled-down warhammer at the alien monster's face. "Aim for its head."

The Marines answered her order with a hail of red blaster fire slamming against the head and neck of the Devil's Hand, but they might as well have been throwing toothpicks at the beast. The monster ignored them and focused, instead, on Vikta. It opened up its giant mouth filled with rows of razor teeth and sent another blast of the strange light at the dragon.

"Gather yourself, Vikta!" Ketrick roared, trying to will the dragon on. "This beast is not stronger than you."

Vikta shook her head free of whatever psychological attack she was under and opened her own mouth. A stream of fire erupted forward, right into the pulsating light coming from the Devil's Hand. It was the strangest, most beautiful thing Riot had ever seen.

The pulsating light from the alien necromancer and the fire from Vikta met in the center like two equal forces vying for dominance. For a moment, an immovable object met an unstoppable force. The area was lit up with a golden light that would have blinded Riot had it not been for the protection of her helmet.

A wild idea came to Riot as she forced herself to look away from the battle and come up with a solution. Once again, she placed her warhammer into its holding clasps on her back. She ran to where a stunned Wang and Rizzo stood a few yards to her right.

"I need whatever Boomballs you have left," Riot said, extending her open hands forward. "All of them."

Both Wang and Rizzo nodded numbly.

Wang gave Riot two Boomballs, both of the explosive variety.

Rizzo handed her one explosive Boomball and another one meant to stun.

Riot held them all in her hand and ran toward where Vikta and the Devil's Hand struggled against one another. When one would take a quick breath, the other would gain ground; the macabre light coming from the Devil's Hand would gain a few yards toward its target when Vikta took a moment to inhale, and visa versa.

The two gladiators were locked in combat, and Riot was going to tip the scales. She looked away from the nexus of their powerful attacks, running toward the Devil's Hand. She unclipped the safety mechanism on one of the explosive Boomballs and pressed the red button on top of the black ball, activating the weapon. The Devil's Hand turned its open mouth her way, four feet above her.

The creature seemed to have de-prioritized Riot and her Marines in favor of taking out the dragon first. Big mistake.

Riot winced as she focused on lobbing the Boomballs into the open gullet of the beast. To her delight, the Boomballs went in one right after the other in quick succession. Like playing some kind of strange carnival game, Riot scored a perfect four for four.

The Boomballs didn't detonate when they came in contact with the alien creature's bizarre white breath. Still, Riot knew her time was up. Even as she turned to run to safety, the explosives detonated in the creature's throat.

Riot was lifted off the ground and thrown through the air like a rag doll. She came crashing down fifteen yards from the explosion. A shower of purple gore, blood, and body parts from the Devil's Hand rained down all over the combatants.

Riot's body ached from the hairs of her head down to the nails on her toes. Her head thrummed with pain. Her ears rang. Riot picked herself up off the ground still being splattered by the entrails of the Devil's Hand.

Her eyes told her two things: that the fight was over, and that she wasn't the only one drenched in the gore. Apparently four Boomballs had been just what the doctor ordered. The upper half of the Devil's Hand was completely gone; only the four legs and the butt end of the creature remained. The short, stocky green tail quivered all on its own.

Rippa was digging herself out from within the demolished building. Vikta and Ketrick were painted with the purple insides of the monster. The dragon was panting, and Ketrick was wiping his eyes free from the purple slime.

"No, don't do it," Wang said over the comms. "Rizzo, don't—"

Riot removed her helmet. The purple gore splattered across her visor was making it difficult to see. She looked to her right where Rizzo had also removed his helmet. His hands were on his knees as he hunched over, ready to puke. Riot couldn't really blame him. They were all covered in the monster's gore from head to foot.

The smell that came with the removal of the helmet didn't help in making her want to keep in her last meal. The scent that wafted toward her nose was something along the lines of stale fish and sweaty armpits, like the smell you got when you hadn't used deodorant for a week, then went for a five mile run on a hot day in the middle of the desert.

"If you puke, it's going to make me—" Wang tried in vain to remove his own helmet. The slippery purple liquid on the outside made it difficult for him to remove it.

Rizzo let loose with a wave of vomit that would have made that little girl in *The Exorcist* stand up and applaud. This was followed by the sound of Wang vomiting over the comms.

"Ugh, that's something we're never going to let you live down." Vet walked up with Doctor Miller at his side. The two were clean of the purple slime, having been too far out on their overwatch position to get hit by the falling organic debris. "Are you okay in there?"

"Oh, jumping Jehosaphat." Doctor Miller placed a hand over the mouth section of her own helmet in disgust as she realized what Wang had just done. "You … you threw up inside your helmet, didn't you?"

"Bahahaha!" Ketrick said, joining the group along with Rippa who arrived in her mech. "Oh, that is so disgusting! Brother Wang, brother Wang, take off your helmet, let's see."

"No, no!" Doctor Miller turned away. "I don't want to see."

Wang finally fought through the sticky mass of purple alien body matter over his helmet and was able to take it off. He looked like he had been involved in a vomit food fight and lost.

"Guys?" Wang looked each of them in the eyes. "I don't ever want to talk about this again."

Even Riot, who had the stomach of a champion, felt queasy looking at him.

"Here." Vet went over to a dead Trilord and ripped off a clean-ish portion of the soldier's shirt. "I think this is going to be funny to always tease you about, but right now, you just look sad."

Ketrick laughed one more time before turning to Riot. "Were you able to take down the Karnayer leader?"

"I wounded him, but he got away," Riot said, shaking her head. "They had a ship hidden behind the warehouse."

"He's going to be pissed that we ruined his little insurrection," Rippa said over her comms. "I should contact the Grovothe high command and see what they've decided about allying with Earth and Hoydren."

"Agreed," Riot said, feeling a sense of doom on the

horizon. "Alveric will strike hard and soon. We need to talk to the Savage Trilords and get their support, as well. Rippa, head back to the ship and make contact. Doctor Miller, let SPEAR know what's going on and that we'll be calling for reinforcements soon. Wang, you go with her and get yourself cleaned up. It's just … it's too much even for me."

Rippa, Doctor Miller, and Wang headed back to the *Valkyrie*, while Riot and the others went back to the center of town where they had spoken with Talon and the other Brute Trilords.

A gathering of brave souls had assembled, with more reinforcements coming in from the surrounding parts of the city. A few dozen Trilords nodded at Riot and the others as they walked forward.

"It's done," Riot said, finding Talon in the crowd. "Whatever past problems you had with the Savage Trilords, I hope you can see that we all share a common enemy now. Not only that, the Savage Trilords, the Grovothe, and yes, even yours truly, humans from Earth, are willing to come to your aid in the time of war."

A few hard stares remained, but most of the Brute's heads nodded along with Riot's words.

Ketrick took the opportunity to speak. "Long have our people fought and died by each other's hands. Perhaps we will do so again one day. But today, we share a common enemy. Maybe it's time to see how truly powerful we can be as one instead of as a house divided."

More mutters of agreement rippled through the gathered crowd.

"Our elected leader was killed by the Karnayers," Talon said, taking a step forward from the crowd. "We'll need time to elect another and make a decision. I can't promise that we will join you, but I can promise that we won't forget what you did here today."

"That will have to be enough," Ketrick said with a slow nod.

Riot was less understanding of Talon's answer. "Well, do what you need to do, quickly. The next time the Karnayers come, it won't be with a handful of soldiers and a single creature. They'll bring an army."

Talon's yellow eyes caught Riot's determined stare, then looked away.

"Let's get back to the ship," Riot said, wiping more purple gore from the front of her armor. "I think—"

"Riot!" Doctor Miller's scream came from the cargo ramp of the *Valkyrie* where she stood, eyes wide with panic. "Come quick!"

9

Riot ran to the rear of the ship, where she was greeted by a frantic Doctor Miller. The doctor's usual friendly visage had been replaced by a mask of horror.

"What is it, Bubbles? Spit it out," Riot said, half-angry, half-frustrated. "What's wrong?"

"I think ... I think you'd better see, there's ... hundreds ... hundreds of them." Doctor Miller turned on her heel and speed walked to the bridge of the *Valkyrie*. "I was about to hail General Armon, when Evonne alerted me to their presence."

By the time Riot and the doctor had entered the bridge, Riot was pretty sure she already knew what they were going to find. Everyone except Wang and Rippa followed them.

"Evonne, show Riot what you showed me," Doctor Miller instructed.

"Immediately," Evonne answered back.

At once, the front window of the *Valkyrie* came alive with a display of space. Even as the image relayed information to Riot, she found herself disbelieving what her eyes were seeing. Hundreds of Karnayer ships floated in orbit above Hoydren, with still more exiting light speed.

Riot recognized the small, maneuverable Scarab fighter ships that were capable of locking on to other space ships and tearing through their hull to unload a crew of Karnayer soldiers. Accompanying these vessels were dozens of transport crafts just like Riot had seen Alveric escape in not more than a half-hour before.

Finally, a massive Karnayer destroyer with black spikes protruding from the hull in varying angles filled the screen.

"Well, had I known he had an army that size, I might have been nicer," Riot said out loud. "Ketrick, I think we're going to need more coffee."

"We're going to need more ships," Vet said to no one and everyone at once. "A lot more ships."

"Evonne, how long until they can attack?" Riot asked.

"If they continue to travel at their current speed, they'll reach Hoydren in the space of ten minutes. Based on the information of tactics used by the House of Karn, they will begin their bombing runs five minutes thereafter."

Riot gave herself the space of a heartbeat to be

surprised. She'd known Alveric would come quickly, just not this quickly.

The next heartbeat had to be spent in action. There was a list of things that needed to be done, people to contact, orders to dole out, and defensive positions to man.

"Rizzo," Riot started, rattling off orders as fast as her lips could relate what her brain was telling her needed to be said. "Get us back to the Savage capital. Vet, contact Colonel Harlan on the screen. Sunshine, tell SPEAR we need them to send everything. Evonne, tell Wang and Rippa I need them on the bridge as fast as their legs can move. Ketrick, do whatever you need to do to convince the Brutes to join the fight."

Everyone besides Ketrick ran to obey. Rizzo ignored the state of his gore-soaked armor and immediately went to the pilot's seat at the front of the ship, starting the engines. Doctor Miller and Vet hit their chairs at their command consoles, following Riot's orders as fast as their fingers would allow.

Ketrick stood beside Riot with a strange smile on his face. He and Vikta had been on the fringe of the gore splatter from the Devil's Hand. Purple splashes decorated his large shoulders and the vest he wore. His red eyes looked deep into Riot's.

"You're very attractive when you order me around," the Trilord prince whispered. He winked at her, then raised his voice to a normal speaking volume. "I will stay and speak with the Brute clan once more, but my place is in the sky with Vikta."

Riot went from being annoyed to being entertained, to being worried all in the space of a few seconds.

"What are you talking about?" She motioned to the screen with both hands. "There are hundreds of ships that will be here within minutes. We need you to stay with the Brutes and get them to come and fight. We'll need all the help we can get."

"The Brutes are not the only faction that has yet to enter this war. I told you before, I am a judge with the ability to speak with the space serpents. Vikta and I will find them and gather a force," Ketrick said as if he were telling Riot what he wanted ordered from a drive-thru menu. "This planet belongs to the space serpents just as much as anyone."

"What are you talking about?" Riot rolled her eyes as an image of Ketrick trying to communicate with an army of dragons raced across her mind. "We stick to the plan, we—"

"I've got Colonel Harlan ready," Vet said as Doctor Miller reported the same about General Armon at the Bulwark.

Wang and Rippa rushed onto the bridge, the former clean and out of his armor, the latter in her tight grey uniform, looking at the screen in front of her, wide-eyed.

"Go and lead, do what you do best," Ketrick said. He leaned in as if he were going to hug her, but put a hand on her shoulder instead. "I'll keep my comm on."

Why do relationships always get in the way of things? Ugh, I hate feeling feelings, Riot thought.

"Go and be careful," Riot said through gritted teeth. "We have a date to keep when this is over."

Ketrick flashed her a grin and ran from the bridge.

If anyone had heard Riot's last words to Ketrick, they didn't say anything. At this point, they had to suspect, if they didn't already know. At least that's what Riot told herself. She bottled her emotions and steeled herself for what was coming next.

"Rippa, contact Admiral Tricon. We'll need the Grovothe if we're going to get through this alive. Wang, you said something about epinephrine shots not too long back. Those are going to come in handy if we have hours of fighting ahead of us." Riot didn't skip a beat as she turned to Vet. "Put Colonel Harlan on the screen, then get Evonne up and running. Right now having robots run the world is looking better than staring down a horde of Karnayers. Oohrah!"

"Oohrah!"

Again, everyone rushed to obey. Rizzo, having waited to offload Ketrick, closed the cargo bay ramp and headed back to the capital city the Savage Trilords. Vet put Colonel Harlan on the screen, then ran with a crazy childlike grin on his face to bring Evonne to life.

"Colonel," Riot said, placing her war hammer by her

command chair as she took a seat. "I'm assuming you've heard the news?"

"Roger that." Colonel Harlan was sitting in his own captain's chair aboard his cruiser class vessel, the *Titan*. "I've been in contact with SPEAR, but General Armon wanted to speak with you directly. We're currently holding a defensive position above the Savage palace. What's your ETA?"

"We're only a few minutes out. Rizzo is punching it as we speak. I have General Armon waiting on the comms now," Riot said as the *Valkyrie* took off like a bullet over Hoydren's dark, jungle-like planet. "We'll see you soon."

"Roger that." Colonel Harlan stared with stern eyes through the screen. Behind him, his crew shouted to one another. "We're enough to hold the line until the cavalry comes, believe that."

"More than enough," Riot said. The screen went blank. A moment later, General Armon's familiar face appeared where Colonel Harlan's had been a moment before.

"Riot," the general started, "we've received the news from Colonel Harlan. The fleet is preparing to leave now. We're bringing everything we've got. We need you to hold out for us, buy us those hours we need to get there. We'll give these sons of guns the fight of their lives."

Both relief and determination coursed over Riot. She was relieved to hear the General was bringing the weight of their resources to bear on the fight. The underground bunker called the Bulwark housed more than a dozen ships of their own. Still, even with the advanced weapons and modification, would that be enough? They would still be outnumbered seven, maybe eight, to one.

Determination gripped her heart at the same time. She was a soldier. If this is what had to be done, then she was the one to do it. It was time to put her money where her mouth was. She was the best in her world, or any other. With her crew behind her, Riot would find a way to succeed, no matter what the cost to herself.

"Riot, are you there?" General Armon's buzz cut, square jaw, and deep stare seemed to soften for a moment. "You and the colonel will find a way."

"We'll be waiting for you when you get here," Riot agreed.

General Armon nodded, then ended the transmission.

"I've got Admiral Tricon," Rippa said from her seat as her fingers maneuvered around the holographic display that popped up above her desk. "Should I put him on?"

"Do it," Riot answered. When had warfare become more about conference calls than pumping rounds into the bad guys?

Admiral Tricon's short, stocky frame popped up on the monitor. He was shouting orders to someone off-screen as he appeared. Riot loved listening to every word coming out of the Grovothe's mouth. "We're not leaving them to face the Karnayers alone. I understand we've only just received the confirmation to ally with Earth but their forces are on Hoydren, and that means that's where we're going!"

Riot waited for her turn to speak.

The grizzled veteran turned his scarred face to her a moment later. "It's good to see you, Riot. I heard you're about to have a Karnayer infestation."

"That we are," Riot said, making a mental note to use a line like that at some point during the fight. "We wanted to extend an invitation your way. We're going to make a party of it. There'll be cookies, punch, and even a photo booth to dress up in and take goofy pictures."

"We've only just received permission to count Earth among our allies," the admiral answered back. "The powers that be are still deciding whether to vote in Hoydren and the Trilords to the alliance or not. Whatever that answer will be, I'm not going to wait. Our human allies are being attacked, and whether they are being attacked on Earth or Hoydren makes no difference in my book. We're en route. Buy us two hours. We have a full squadron of fighters ready to tear into the Karnayers."

In a few hours they could be dead.

But Riot silenced the voice in her head that

whispered thoughts of fear and doubt. They were going to hold out. They had to.

"Roger that," Riot said over the screen. Despite the hour, she couldn't help smiling. "It's good to see you, Admiral. I'm looking forward to teaming up with you again."

"As am I." Then Admiral Tricon spat another series of growl-like orders to someone off-screen before the monitor went black. "All available mech units are to be piloted—that means all of them!"

"All we have to do is hold out for a few hours," Rippa said quietly as if she were convincing herself it was possible. "Admiral Tricon will be here then, and a few hours later, General Armon will arrive."

Riot understood what Rippa was doing. She, too, was running through the odds of their survival against hundreds of Karnayer ships and ignoring the outcome.

"Evonne, I need everyone on the bridge ASAP," Riot said. "Congrats on your new body, as well. I was going to say you deserved it, but truth is, you just bugged us enough."

"Thank you," a voice said from behind Riot. "I've just notified them."

Riot turned in her seat to see the robotic body Vet and Doctor Miller had created for Evonne standing on the bridge. Her long, raven-black hair was perfect, as was the rest of her fair complexion.

A grinning Vet appeared behind Evonne. Doctor

Miller rose from her seat with a smile as she looked over their work.

Wang ran onto the bridge a moment later, googly-eyed as he took in Evonne's new form.

"Let's focus, people," Riot said, looking out through the window of the ship as Hoydren's lush vegetation raced past them. "It's time to go to work."

10

The bridge sat quiet as Rizzo piloted them back to the Savage Trilord city. As he slowed down their forward momentum, the gigantic moon of the alien city showed them exactly where the battle would take place. The Savage Trilord's capital sat on a high hill. On top of the hill was a giant, square pyramid. Below it, down the sides of the hill, were everything from homes, to barracks, to stores.

Colonel Harlan's cruiser class ship, the *Titan*, hovered high over the city in a defensive position. All alone in the vast skyline dotted with stars, it seemed lonely, or maybe that's just how Riot felt at the moment and she was projecting her own feelings onto the situation.

City evacuations were still taking place for all of the Savage Trilord children. Riot could see tiny figures running through the night. Torches and fires throughout the city lit their way. Even smaller shadows followed the children.

"I should be down there," Rippa said, looking over to Riot. "We'll need every gun we can get capable of firing at the oncoming Scarab ships. The weapons on my mech can take them down if they get close enough."

"We have two Firebreath A9s in the armory," Vet said with his constant scowl that somehow seemed deeper at the moment. "We can send them with Rippa, who can dole them out to Killa and her army. There're only two rocket launchers, but they're the only weapons we have that are capable of taking down ships."

"Do it," Riot said, looking from Vet to Rippa. "Take your mech and the Firebreaths with you. We'll hold the line with you from up here."

Rippa nodded and moved to leave. She hesitated for a moment, then turned to look everyone in the eyes. "I realize I've only known you all for short time, but you all have my respect. No one dies alone. If we burn, then we all burn together."

The strength and pure determination in Rippa's voice quieted any response. She left the bridge, already on her way to her armored mech unit.

"Is it just me, or were her last words unnecessarily dark?" Doctor Miller shook her head. "I don't want to burn. Do you want to burn? We could still win this fight."

"We will," Wang said from his seat beside her. "If anyone can, it's us."

"Evonne," Riot said, ignoring the talk between Doctor Miller and Wang. "How much time do we have until the Karnayers arrive at the city?"

"Two minutes, perhaps more if they take extra time to coordinate their attack," Evonne replied without any hesitation. Her new physical face looked at Riot, unblinking, like she was staring into Riot instead of just looking at her.

"Evonne." Riot shook her head. "You're going to have to blink when you talk to me. You're really freaking me out with that deadpan stare. I have enough going on at the moment."

"Oh, right," Evonne said, batting her eyes as if she had a contact falling out. "Sorry, is this better?"

"Maybe a bit less. You—"

"We're getting hailed by Colonel Harlan," Doctor Miller interrupted. "Sorry, I didn't mean to cut you off."

"It's okay. Put him on," Riot said as she felt Rizzo maneuver the *Valkyrie* to the ground to let Rippa off.

The screen came to life a moment later and Colonel Harlan's familiar face appeared on the ship's bridge. "Riot, I see you're already offloading your mech unit with the two Firebreaths you have on board. We already gave our two to Killa and the rest of the Trilords."

"Yeah, at least we'll have some help from the

ground," Riot said, trying to be optimistic even though everything in her body told her otherwise. "Even if they can take some of the fire off of us, it'll help."

"Agreed." Colonel Harlan actually grinned. "You and your crew have the only experience of fighting the Karnayers. I thought you should be the one to set us right. I have the Karnayers making their approach in under two minutes now. I'll put you on our main screen so my crew can hear you, as well."

Riot licked dry lips, and the screen in front of her widened to a view of the *Titan's* bridge. Nervous eyes looked back at her, waiting for her to give them the words of courage they would need to see them through the fight.

Fear, doubt, despair, and a dozen other feelings were crashing inside of her, begging her to be the person she once was before; the woman who allowed herself to succumb to her weaknesses, whether it be emotional or addiction, was fighting to be heard.

Riot wasn't that person anymore.

"We can bet on the Karnayer Scarabs providing the main assault on us, as well as on the city. They're fast but weak, and will probably try to latch on to our ships before they shoot us out of the air," Riot said, standing up from her captain's chair. "More than likely, the destroyer will stay in upper orbit, waiting for our reinforcements. We can expect transport ships coming in while the Scarabs keep us busy, and we'll have to allow that, for now. The main priority is keeping the ships off of the evacuating city. There are kids down there."

Riot took a breath. Her adrenaline was already beginning to flow with the promise of the fight to come. Talking was getting harder as her heart raced to meet the challenge. She took a brief moment, looking at her own crew, and then at the Marines on board the *Titan*.

"This is our time," Riot said, adding strength to her words as her voice heightened in volume. "The Karnayers are expecting to roll right over us and destroy the city. I say we give them a fight they've never seen. I say we will hold this line until reinforcements arrive. I say it doesn't matter how many they have on their side, because there is not a fighting force in the universe like the Marines. We hold to give the fleeing children of Hoydren time to live another day!"

"Oohrah!" the crew on the screen and her own Marines on the bridge shouted in unison.

"We hold for a future free of monsters!"

"Oohrah!"

"We hold for the brothers and sister besides us!"

"Oohrah!"

"We hold!"

"Oohrah!"

"We hold!"

"Oohrah!"

The intensity on the bridge was palpable, and Riot's

heart beat like a war drum. She had managed to get the words out despite the level of adrenaline pumping through her veins.

"We're with you," Colonel Harlan said. "Here they come. Don't give them an inch!"

With that, the screen went back to showing a view of the dark night sky. Rizzo lifted the ship from the ground once more, having already set down Rippa and her mech.

"Before the party starts, I want you all to know I've had a blast traveling into space with all of you." Riot couldn't help a grin that twitched at the corners of her lips. "From Vet and his diapers, to Rizzo and Wang throwing up, from smearing what they thought were Ketrick's ancestors across their face. Oh yeah, and Sunshine, you threw up, too, right? What was it? A big breakfast before travel?"

Her crew chuckled around the bridge as images brought from Riot's words came to mind.

Here They Come, Rizzo said, writing big red letters across the screen, ones that disappeared a moment later.

Riot directed her attention to the main screen. Barely visible through the night sky, hundreds of Scarab ships screamed toward them.

"Did you have some party favors to give out?" Riot asked, looking over to Wang.

"I do." Wang removed his stare from the oncoming enemy and went around placing three augmented epinephrine pens near each person on the ship. "Take them one at a time when you need a jolt of energy. It should feel like injecting espresso directly into your heart."

"Awesome," Vet said, placing his in a side compartment in the leg of his armor. "I freaking love espresso."

Riot accepted hers, staring down the charging enemy. They had seconds before the conflict would begin. "Evonne, we're going to need you to go to the armory and bring as many weapons as you can carry to the bridge. Bubbles, go with her—bring everything. When the Scarab ships latch on to us, we'll need the firepower up here to keep them away from the bridge."

"Gotcha," Doctor Miller whispered as she tore her eyes away from the coming enemy.

Evonne and the doctor left the bridge at a run.

"Here we go, Wolves. Let's do what we do best," Riot said as Rizzo prepared to begin his defensive maneuvers. The ships were nearly within firing distance. "We've got the best pilot in the universe with us. Let's bring the pain."

Green rounds erupted from the first line of Scarab ships coming at them. Rizzo punched the thrusters, sending them above the first volley.

"Wang, take the main guns," Riot shouted to her left. "Vet, I need you to work some magic and take whatever power you can from unnecessary features and put them into the shields."

"Roger," both men said in unison.

Wang let loose with the twin blasters on the *Valkyrie* that shot red weapons fire into the oncoming Scarab throng. Rizzo maneuvered the ship in the air like it was an extension of his own hand.

"Vet, it's feeling pretty quiet in here," Riot said to her XO. "Let's hear some sound."

Vet didn't have to ask her what she meant. He took a minute to allow the sound from the blasts outside to enter the bridge before putting on a familiar song by a band named Rage Against the Machine.

The bass in the song added an extra layer of focus as the enemy ships screamed around them. There were so many Scarabs, it was impossible for Wang to miss.

BOOM! BOOM! BOOM!

Nearly every one of their shots hit an enemy, but for every ship that exploded, it seemed another took its place. Rizzo did his best to harass the ships, staying away from the bulk of the enemy as much as he could. But they were everywhere. Fighting the ships was like a dog biting at a swarm of bees; no matter how many they swatted from the sky, more came.

The *Valkyrie* shuddered as green blaster fire struck the ship's shields. Riot gritted her teeth.

"Shields at ninety percent," Vet said from his seat to Riot's right. "I can pull some power to the shields from the non-essential ship operations, but it's only a matter of time before they break through."

"Do it," Riot said, praying they would be able to

hold out long enough for the Grovothe to arrive. "Whatever you need to do to keep her in the air."

"Roger that," Vet said.

Rizzo took them through a mass of Scarab ships that battered them with fire. Wang shot down another half-dozen. Their view over the Hoydren landscape turned from dark sky and foliage to one of the Trilord city. Scarabs were starting their attack runs over the city on the hill.

Red beams of laser fire came from the four Firebreaths stationed around the city. To Riot's surprise and amazement, Rippa had positioned her mech on the very top of the square pyramid capital building on the top of the hill. Her mech was firing heated metal gauss rounds from both cannons mounted on its forearms, as well as the blue laser beam that came from its helmet.

Rippa's location was perfect for gaining the attention of the Scarabs and directing them away from the main section of the city, but on the other hand, her mech was taking an extreme amount of enemy fire.

"Rizzo—" Riot said, cutting off her own words as her pilot read her mind and brought the *Valkyrie* over Rippa's mech. Wang lit up another three Scarab ships as they passed over Rippa. Two of the Scarab crafts exploded right there, while the third spiraled out of control and fell, crashing down to the jungle interior.

"We're back," Doctor Miller said, gasping as she reentered the bridge. She carried Rizzo's Vulcan in both hands, heaving it like an oversized piece of luggage. "How do you lift this thing when you're fighting? It weighs more than … well, I don't know how much it weighs. It weighs a lot."

Evonne followed the doctor onto the bridge, her arms loaded down with everything from Destroyer T9 shotguns to Villain Pulse rifles and molten blades. The stack of weaponry was piled so high in her arms, Riot couldn't even see her face.

"Did you make Evonne super strong, as well?" Riot didn't take her eyes off the robot as Evonne gently placed the pile of weapons down beside Riot's seat.

"As strong as Rippa's mech, and blaster proof," Vet said, maneuvering his hands around the holographic display that popped up at his station. "Shield is at seventy percent."

The *Valkyrie* shook violently. Riot had experienced that feeling before, a few times. She knew what that shudder meant. Rizzo confirmed her suspicion with a quick line of text across the screen: **Scarabs on the hull.**

11

"**R**oger that." Riot jumped up from her seat. As she did, she saw Colonel Harlan's craft, the *Titan*, flash by their ship's window. They were giving more than they got, but they, too, looked like some kind of small animal batting away a swarm of gnats. "Vet, you take the guns and the shields. Wang and Evonne, with me."

"What … what do I do?" Doctor Miller asked, looking on with wide eyes.

Riot motioned to the doctor's helmet that sat beneath her chair on the bridge. "Get your helmet on and pick up that Vulcan you dragged in here. We'll bolt shut the doors to the bridge. Anything that gets through, you light it up like it's the Fourth of July."

Wang transferred the controls to Vet before getting up from his seat. He slammed his own helmet down on his head before picking up a Villain Pulse Rifle from the stock pile. He placed it over his shoulder before grabbing a molten blade and a Destroyer T9.

"I … I don't know if I can do this," Doctor Miller said, shaking as she reached for her helmet. "I mean, I'm … I'm a scientist, not a soldier."

Riot forwent the molten blade, but also picked up a Villain Pulse Rifle. She swung the weapon onto her back, along with her war hammer. Next, she grabbed the stocky grips of a Destroyer T9.

Another shudder hit the *Valkyrie*.

"We've got another Scarab ship right next to the first," Vet said from his station on the bridge. "The first is already unloading soldiers. They landed in the training and weight room."

"Got it." Riot looked to a frightened Doctor Miller. She placed a heavy hand onto the woman's shoulder. "You will do it, because you're stronger than you know. You proved that in the Zenoth hive. You're Vet's and Rizzo's defense. I know you won't let them down."

Doctor Miller looked at the men behind her who were busy at the controls of the ship, slowly nodding. She placed her helmet onto her head. "I'm not going to let anything happen to them."

"I know you won't," Riot said, motioning to Wang and Evonne. "Let's go."

The two Marines and the robot exited the bridge.

"Evonne, seal the bridge," Riot said, placing her still-purple-gore-stained helmet on her head.

"Done," Evonne said with a light whoosh behind them as the bridge doors sealed shut.

"You don't need a weapon?" Riot asked Evonne as she lifted the Destroyer in front of her as the trio made their way to the exercise room. "I know you're blaster proof and all, but really, weapons help in a fight."

"I'm not going to let anything happen to you or Corporal Wang," Evonne said in such a matter-of-fact way, Riot believed her. "I have a physical body now. I'm going to shield you. The two of you can take cover behind me."

"I think I'm in love," Wang said through the comms in his helmet. "Is that weird?"

"Not now," Riot said as she allowed Evonne to take point. She lifted the Destroyer over the right side of the robot's shoulder. Wang did the same on Evonne's left.

The group made their way to the exercise room without encountering any Karnayer soldiers, thus far.

"They are massing en force," Evonne reported. "Perhaps they are waiting for another Scarab ship or two to make contact with our ship before attacking at once."

"Well, let's not give them the—"

The *Valkyrie* quivered again. Much more than it should have, had it only been hit by another round of enemy fire.

Vet's voice came through the comms again. "Shields aren't able to keep off the Scarabs, only the blaster fire. Two more Scarabs have connected to the hull right along side the first two. Shields at fifty percent and falling fast."

"You and Rizzo worry about taking as many out of the sky as you can," Riot replied. "We'll take care of the Karnayer soldiers already in the ship."

"Four ships now," Wang said out loud. "Six enemies to a ship. That's means we're up against twenty-four alien baddies."

The group rounded a corner. Down the hall and to the right, the door to the exercise room stood wide open.

"I think it's time to take a hit of one of those epinephrine shots you hooked us up with," Riot said to Wang. She had ignored the level of exhaustion and fatigue her body felt from not only being up all night but also already having fought a battle earlier that evening.

With her right hand, Riot reached for a compartment built into the right side of her leg armor. She looked down at what she was doing long enough to smell the purple gore on her armor and see the abuse her protection had already taken.

"Cheers?" Wang lifted his one blue vial into the space in front of his helmet. The vial looked like a test tube with a needle on one end and a thumb depressor on the other. "This probably isn't a good time to warn you of the side effects, is it?"

"Side effects?" Riot repeated the words as she

clinked one of the three epinephrine shots she had against Wang's. "What side effects?"

"Oh, you know, the usual," Wang said as if he were some kind of pharmaceutical commercial. "Severe itching in the nether regions, temporary loss of taste, swelling in your tongue, hard of hearing, dry eyes, club foot, hangnails, warts, a severe case of the mumbles, and anal leakage. There are some other ones I forgot."

Boots slamming against the floor hall and shouts from the Karnayer troops interrupted whatever Riot was going to say.

"Do it, and if I get anal leakage from this, so help me God, Wang," Riot said as she drove the syringe into a spot in her abdomen where a blaster round had left a small opening in her armor.

Riot pushed the plunger with her thumb. The feeling was a brief prick of pain, followed by the strongest rush of energy Riot had ever felt. It was like liquid electricity coursing through every inch of her body. Her eyes widened, her heart rate doubled, and she had the urge to move—and move fast.

The sensation came at the perfect time. The four Scarab ships full of Karnayers had gathered in force and came charging from around the corner. They came so fast, they nearly collided with Evonne who, true to her word, took a shield-like stance in front of Riot and Wang.

Blaster fire lit up the hall. The Karnayers opened up on Evonne, who waded through the green bolts of energy like she was some kind of bulldozer traveling though a hailstorm.

Riot's trigger finger was a blur as she aimed around Evonne and mowed down the enemy with her Destroyer T9. The Syndicate weapon modified by SPEAR was like a tommy gun married to a Benelli shotgun. It sprayed a volley of red blaster fire at the enemy, chewing through their black armor and helmets.

The pure focus in Riot aided by the epinephrine shot made her duck and roll out of the way from the incoming fire. Although Evonne was taking the bulk of it, green blaster rounds were still managing to find their way to Riot and Wang.

"Use Evonne as cover," Riot shouted into her comms as she ducked and weaved through the blasts. She sent another burst of fire that hit a Karnayer in the chest and sent him reeling backwards into his comrades. "Don't let them catch you standing still."

"What!" Wang shouted, still firing his own weapon and moving just as quickly as Riot.

"I said keep moving!" Riot repeated.

"What! Who's chewing?" Wang shouted so loud into his comms, it made Riot's ears ring.

Riot remembered one of the side effects of the augmented epinephrine shots being hearing loss. It seemed Wang was suffering one of the signs now. Riot wondered if anal leakage was coming next.

Watching Evonne wade into the Karnayers was

epic. The robotic AI took blaster fire point-blank and kept moving forward. The Karnayers who lived past the initial engagement were starting to understand this black-haired woman who didn't blink could not be taken down with their weapons. Instead of trying to push past her, they backpedaled down the hall, ducking back into the exercise room, around corners, and into doorways of other rooms.

Evonne stalked after them like a terminator on a search-and-destroy mission.

Riot and Wang followed, blasting at anything that moved.

Riot tracked along with her weapon at incredible speed. If she were capable of slowing down, she might have, but at the moment, the drugs screaming in her system demanded action.

BAM! BAM! BAM!

Wang took out a Karnayer peeking around the corner to their right. Riot took out two more on the left. A green blaster round caught Wang square on the helmet, sending him stumbling backwards. He struck the ground hard and didn't move.

"Wang! Wang!" Riot backpedaled and knelt next to her corporal. "Wang, you have to get up!"

"What!?" Wang shouted back, sitting up from his spot. He reached for the Villain Pulse Rifle on his back as he readied himself to return to the fight. "Who? Has what?"

"Fight!" Riot said as she was struck in the torso and

the right shoulder. She grimaced past the pain as the rounds took her breath away, causing temporary pain that her nanites would soon repair. "Fight!"

The remaining Karnayers were wising up to Evonne's impenetrability and began changing tactics. Small disks the size of hockey pucks slid across the floor. They landed feet from Evonne, who was in the lead.

"Get down!" Evonne shouted as she spread her arms and legs, trying to create a larger shield between the explosive and the marines.

BAM!

Riot wasn't really sure where she landed as she tried to struggle to her feet again. All she remembered was the grenades going off, then being flung into the air so hard she slammed through a door into the weight room, and finally sliding to a halt.

Neither Wang nor Evonne were in the room with her. Riot's ears were ringing like they never had before. Her armor had held up well under the blast, but burning pain lanced around her body where her armor had already been exposed by previous shots.

Her Destroyer was gone somewhere, lost in the mix. She unslung the pulse rifle from her back to find it still in working order. As the smoke settled near the entrance to the room, a movement caught her eye. Riot rose to one knee, looking down the sight of her weapon. Two Karnayers were using a helmetless Wang as a shield.

Wang was bleeding from his nose and his lip. Swelling was forming and healing was taking place around his right eye as Riot looked down her scope. The Karnayer directly behind Wang held a small firearm to his head. The other behind the two pointed a rifle at Riot.

"Drop your weapon, or we'll blow his brains into the next galaxy, human scum," ordered the Karnayer directly behind Wang. "Do it—*now*."

12

"That was disappointing," Riot said as she took a breath and aimed down her sights. "I thought I was just going to be able to shoot whatever came at me through the door. You know, kinda like when you get the mail, all excited something interesting might be coming, but it's just bills?"

"What are you talking about?" the other Karnayer said through this helmet, as he pointed his weapon at Riot,. His voice sounded stressed, like he sensed some kind of trap. "Lower your weapon, or you both die—now!"

"I'm going to have to take a hard pass on that," Riot said.

BOOM! BOOM!

The Karnayers behind Wang didn't even have a chance. They fell at the same time as Riot's two shots hit them, a millisecond apart. Her aim was perfect. Twin smoking holes had blossomed from the center of their helmets.

"You could have shot me!" Wang jumped away from the dead Karnayers, feeling his body with his hands for the signs of an entry wound.

"I was willing to take that chance," Riot said, handing her weapon to Wang as she unslung her warhammer from her back. "Besides, you would have healed."

"Not if you shot me in the face!" Wang yelled again, unable to hear how loud he really was.

"It would have been an improvement on your features." Riot grinned under her helmet and moved past. "Want to take a look at the halls?"

Evonne stood over a pile of broken Karnayer bodies. Her clothing was ripped to shreds, circuitry showing under her skin in a handful of different places. Half of the skin on her face had been ripped away, along with her right hand. Underneath the fake skin, a metal skeleton reminded Riot of a machine. A series of sparks fell down Evonne's back.

"The Karnayers are gone, but I seem to have taken damage from the grenade—seem to have taken damage from the grenade." Evonne's Australian accent failed for a moment as she spoke so slowly it sounded like a song on half speed.

"Riot, are you okay back there?" Vet asked over the comms. "We heard an explosion."

"We're still here," Riot said as Evonne twitched and Wang pounded his right ear with his glove. "We're okay-ish."

"Good," Vet said in a strained tone that worried Riot. "Because we've got trouble. We need you on the bridge, ASAP."

"En route," Riot said over her comms. She motioned for Evonne and Wang to follow. "Let's go. Back to the bridge."

"Why … why do you keep looking at me like that—like that?" Evonne asked Riot as she gave her a last glance before jogging back to the bridge.

"Because you're doing that whole not blinking thing again," Riot said, shaking her head. "And half the skin is peeled back from your face."

Riot jogged back to the bridge with the AI and Wang in tow. She remembered how much Evonne had held true to her promise and took the brunt of the blow from the Karnayers, and a little voice inside her head that had somehow begun to grow in volume since she started the whole space travel thing told her she should say something nice.

"But you worked well as a shield," Riot said, replacing her warhammer on her back and taking off her helmet. "I mean, for a robot, you did well."

"Thank yo—thank you," Evonne said, and if robots could sound happy, she did. "I'll try to blink—I'll try to blink more in the future."

The energy from the epinephrine pen had died in

Riot's body now and the familiar fatigue had crept back in. It seemed Wang's little miracle drugs shone bright, but not for very long.

"Why does everyone need freaking words of affirmation around here?" Riot said as she stepped next to the closed doors of the bridge. "Evonne, open the doors."

Evonne stepped forward, still sparking from the wounds she had taken in the fight. The doors to the bridge opened a moment later.

"I am not a victim!" Doctor Miller opened fire with the Vulcan. A wild spray of red rounds careened all around Riot, Evonne, and Wang as the doctor let out a mild war cry that sounded more like a whimper.

A second later, Doctor Miller released her hold in the trigger and dropped her weapon.

"Oh, my gosh." Doctor Miller tore off her helmet and ran to see if she had hit anyone. "I'm so sorry, Riot, I'm so sorry! I thought you were the Karnayers coming for Rizzo and Vet. I wasn't going to let them get taken alive."

"You were going to kill them?" Wang said from his spot behind Evonne, where he had taken cover when Doctor Miller opened fire. "That's what that saying means."

"Oh, gosh no." Doctor Miller looked even more panicked than before. "I just mean I was going to protect them and not let them get shot in the back."

Riot was about to lay into the doctor, when a shout from Vet drew her attention.

"I didn't want to worry you before, but shields are at ten percent." Vet gritted his teeth at his control panel. "Another shot, and we'll be wide open."

Rizzo still maneuvered the craft like the expert pilot he was, but it was clear the extra weight of the four Scarab ships in their hull were weighing them down. Riot looked out at the screen to see hundreds of the small Karnayer ships still permeating the night sky. A distant glow of the two rising Hoydren suns told her how close to morning they were.

"Can you send any more power to the shields?" Riot placed her warhammer by her command chair and took a seat. "How is the *Titan* faring?"

"I've sent everything I can to the shields already," Vet said, grimacing as he looked over to Riot. "The *Titan* is in as bad a spot as we're in."

The *Valkyrie* shook again. This time, sparks flew through the air and a small fire broke out behind Vet's command console.

"Shields are gone!" Vet yelled as he looked to the others still standing. "Strap in! The next hit is going to take us down."

Wang, Doctor Miller, and even a sparking Evonne, obeyed Vet's words and raced to find their seats.

Riot did the same, bringing the harness down on either side of her shoulders to a clasp that came up from the bottom of the seat.

BOOM!

The *Valkyrie* shuddered like a whale in its death throes.

We're going down, Rizzo said over the main screen.

Riot's stomach clenched, then raced up to her chest as the thruster in the *Valkyrie* died and the ship began to glide instead of fly.

"Rawww!" Vet still made use of the guns as he lit the night sky with red blaster fire. Riot saw him take out at least two more Scarabs as they went down toward the alien planet's jungle floor.

Why didn't you just go out on a date with him? Riot was surprised to have her final thoughts be on Ketrick. *Because you're still damaged goods from the past. Because you don't want to open up again. Well, now you'll never get to open up to anyone. Hope you're happy.*

The weightless feeling hit Riot again and snapped her out of her own train of thought while the *Valkyrie* continued to lose altitude. Rizzo, being the ace pilot he was, maneuvered the ship away from the city and toward the jungle to the south.

The ship scraped the tops of the jungle trees, its lush green-and-purple foliage just visible in the morning light. Riot braced herself for the impact, but her mind was now on her crew.

"Heads between your knees!" Riot yelled as the ship lost more altitude and began battering down the trees and shrubbery on the jungle floor.

The *Valkyrie* broke itself on the many thick trunks of the Hoydren jungle. It slammed into the ground so hard, Riot thought for sure she'd have cracked teeth. The *Valkyrie* continued to slide along the Hoydren jungle floor until it finally came to a stop at the base of a giant rock.

Riot blinked past the smoke coming from a dozen different fires on the bridge. Wires had been torn loose from overhead compartments, and sparking electric panels and fuses blown by the impact were hazards all on their own, but none of that mattered to Riot. Her crew needed to come first.

Smoke burned Riot's lungs as she unhooked herself from her seat. She was lucky the *Valkyrie* had remained in one piece. Her view outside the front window was nothing more than the jungle interior.

Riot fell to the ground once her harness had been unlocked, still coughing from the smoke. A burning, itching feeling clawed at her eyes as she looked for her helmet. Somewhere in the event of the crash, it had been lost.

Out of the white-and-grey smoke, Rizzo came with an unconscious Doctor Miller in his arms. His eyes were watering, but he looked like he was in one piece.

Riot fought to her feet, keeping her head low to avoid as much of the smoke as possible. "Vet, Wang!"

"I'm here, I'm here!" Vet came in from her right. A metal piece of paneling stuck out of the right side of his body like an open panel showing off the inside of his guts. "I know, I know I have to take this thing out, but let's get out of here first."

The smoke was so thick, Riot couldn't see far enough to her left to make out Wang and Evonne. She was almost on top of them when she found them. Evonne had taken a protective stance over Wang, shielding him from any further debris. Apart from a line of dark red blood that came from the left side of Wang's head, he didn't look any the worse for wear.

"On your feet." Riot coughed into her hand as she led her group from the bridge. "Let's get out of here before we all die of smoke inhalation."

Riot grabbed Wang around his shoulders to help him out of his seat and through the *Valkyrie* to the cargo bay door.

"Evonne, are we in any danger of the ship exploding?" Riot asked as she blinked through the hot tears brought on by the smoke.

"No. The ship has undergone major damage; however, we are not in immediate threat of a—we are not in immediate threat of an explosion," Evonne said as she walked with the others, impervious to the smoke. "I've also opened the exterior hatches and cargo bay doors to help with the smoke. I'm trying to get the emergency systems back online to quell the fires. They were diverted to the shields previously."

"Good," Riot said as her group reached the cargo bay doors. "I'm going to need you to gather our helmets and weapons while we get to the exit."

"Of course—of course." Evonne stopped mid-stride, looking at Riot while she blinked so many times, it looked like she had something in her eye. "I am so glad I have a body now so I can help you—help you better."

"Yeah, okay," Riot said as she and the rest of her unit made it to the jungle outside of the smoke-filled interior of the ship.

Riot let Wang walk under the power of his own two feet. He went to go look at Doctor Miller, who was still unconscious as Rizzo set her down to the right of the ship.

Riot spat the taste of charcoal and smoke from her mouth as her eyes took in the devastation. A deep landing trek had been punctured into the ground of the Hoydren jungle. As far as her eye could see, a lane of dark brown soil had been churned up by the downed *Valkyrie*. Foliage to either side of the lane burned as tiny flames tried to consume the dense brush of the jungle.

A scream lit up the sky as a unit of Scarab ships circled Riot and her crew. Four of the dark, pointed crafts hovered around her and her defenseless men.

Before Riot could decide whether to try to run back inside the burning *Valkyrie*, or to just stand there and give them the single finger salute, a roar filled the sky.

13

R iot already knew what the sound was, and despite her situation, a smile cracked her lips. The four Scarab ships hovering above her shifted in the sky as their pilots moved to meet this new threat.

Riot lifted her right hand to shield her eyes from the bright morning suns still cresting the horizon. Dozens of tiny dots formed in front of the bright light as flying beasts took shape.

"Riot, come in, Riot!" Colonel Harlan's voice cracked over the comms. By the sound of his voice, Riot knew he had been trying to raise her for a while. "What is your status? We saw your ship go down."

Thanks to the nanites embedded into Riot, she had access to communications, even without her helmet.

"I'm here," Riot said, not taking her eyes off the scene of a dozen dragons joining the fight. A sense of joy and pride filled her heart. She couldn't make them out yet, but she knew Ketrick and Vikta were leading the charge.

"What's your status and, well … are you seeing what I'm seeing?"

"Our ship's out of commission, but we'll make it," Riot said, looking over at Wang, who was helping a now-conscious Doctor Miller into a sitting position. "And yes, I'm seeing what you're seeing. Our allies have joined the fight."

"Roger that," Colonel Harlan said. His voice sounded half-stressed, half-full of wonder. "We've taken more damage than we have a right to. I don't know how the *Titan* is still in the air. We've lost forward thrusters and have to set down inside the city walls."

Riot understood what he was saying without actually saying it. Colonel Harlen and the *Titan* would not be able to make it to pick up Riot and her crew. They would have to trek through the jungle on their own, back to the city.

"Roger that." Riot eyed the Scarabs that seemed uncertain what to do next. "We'll make it back. You hold that city."

The four Scarabs floating above Riot seemed to have received their own orders in the interim. As one, they raced toward the group of dragons, who were maneuvering through the air, turning their flames and claws on the Scarab ships.

"You there, Sorceress?" Ketrick's familiar voice sounded in Riot's ear. His voice was distant and strained, but strong.

"You joined the party just in time," Riot said, unable to keep a smile from her lips. "Looks like you managed to convince a few of the dragons to join the fight."

"We'll hold them for as long as we can," Ketrick grunted. Wind whipped through the comms, making his voice static-laced and almost unrecognizable. "I saw the *Valkyrie* go down. Get to the city."

As much as Riot wanted to stay on the comms with Ketrick, she understood he was in the fight of his life. Even with a dozen full-grown dragons at his command, he was still vastly outnumbered.

"We'll be fine," Riot said. For a second, she considered not saying what she wanted to next. Who knew who might be listening over the comms? A second later, she was reminded of her regret as the *Valkyrie* crashed to the jungle floor. "You get yourself back safe. We have a date to go on."

"Yes, we do," Ketrick said.

Riot could picture the goofy grin on his face as he mouthed the words.

Evonne, returning from the smoking *Valkyrie*, tore Riot from her fond memories of the man she knew she was beginning to love.

"I gathered helmets, weapons, and as many supplies as I could carry—I could carry," Evonne said, twitching as more sparks erupted from the back of her neck.

"Shall I go in to collect more supplies—collect more supplies?"

"No, you did good," Riot said, looking down at the pile of items Evonne had brought. She had carried as much as three Marines' worth on her single trip. "Wolves, let's gear up and head out."

"Roger," Vet grunted as he tore out the piece of blood-soaked metal from his leg.

Wang, Vet, Rizzo, and Doctor Miller grouped around the pile of supplies. Helmets were placed on heads, weapons checked, and supply packs shouldered.

While the group geared up, everyone's line of sight was on the battle taking place in the sky. Ketrick had brought his dragons to bear on the enemy more than a mile from the Savage Trilord capital. Winged serpents ranging in color from burnt orange, to deep purple, to ebony black, maneuvered through the morning sky like no ship ever could. Fire erupted from their mouths. They caught Scarab ships in their claws and tore them apart.

The green blaster fire from the ships that managed to find the dragons did nothing more than infuriate the beasts. It seemed dragon hide was able to withstand even a ship's blaster. How long the dragons would be able to battle against the overwhelming odds was something else entirely.

Riot placed her warhammer on her back and hefted a Villain Pulse Rifle. Sleep was something to be envied at the moment. With the city under siege, who knew when any of them would get their next chance for some shut-eye?

Worry and fear scratched at the back of Riot's mind. She knew how to quell their screams of insolence, but there was an old enemy she still struggled with.

"Vet, see if you can get Sparky over here to stop repeating her words." Riot nodded to Evonne, who was blinking like a maniac. "Wang, check out Doctor Miller one more time before we move out. Rizzo, hit up Rippa and tell her what's going on."

Riot moved back into the ship as her men began performing their duties.

"Where're you going Riot?" Doctor Miller asked as she lowered her head for Wang to examine.

"Don't worry, I'll be right back," Riot said, not answering the doctor's question. She made her way up the open cargo bay ramp and through the now-less-smoky interior of the ship.

With the exterior ports open to allow the smoke to escape and the emergency system back online thanks to Evonne, the fires were now out with only the smell of smoke on the air.

Riot shoved out of her mind the idea of what she was about to do. Her steps carried her through the interior of the ship and to the mess hall, where she touched the screen of the food dispenser closest to the door. She cycled through the options until she reached the alcohol list and punched in her order for the mind-numbing liquid.

I just need one drink to set me straight, Riot said to herself. *One drink will be fine, and I'll be back outside. I deserve it. I need it.*

A glass full of the amber whiskey appeared in the cove below the ordering screen. Riot's mouth watered as her hand hovered above the cup.

Motion in the doorway to the mess hall made Riot shift her attention. Vet stood there with his ever-present scowl. His right eye wearing the metal eye patch was covered with black smoke that made him look like a pirate.

For a moment, Riot stared at Vet. Vet looked from the glass next to Riot, and then to her.

"Vet, I—"

Vet shook his head, looking down at the floor. "I just came to say that Evonne is ready to go, as well as Doctor Miller. Rizzo reached Rippa. Her mech is in bad shape, but she's making do with what she's got. I was going to see if you wanted me to grab anything else from the ship before we began the trek to the city."

"Good," Riot said, feeling heat rise to her face. If she was honest with herself, she was almost happy she was found out instead of having to sneak around. "I'll be right out."

"Roger." Vet turned like he was about to leave, and then turned back, his scowl present while he stared down at the floor. "You've saved all of us now. All of us owe you our lives. Rizzo would be dead if you hadn't pulled him out of that crashed chopper, Wang would still be in the brig, and I'd be in the ground, too, if you hadn't saved me during the Afghanistan campaign."

"Vet, you don't need to bring up the past," Riot said, wondering why her XO was talking about these events in the first place.

"I'm saying all of this because you're the strongest person I know. By that, I mean Marine, alien, or whatever else we've come into contact with." Vet's single eye began to water like he was about to cry, yet his voice never faltered. "I'm saying this, because you're the best person I know by yourself, without the help or comfort of anything. You've always been enough. Rizzo, Wang, me, even Doctor Miller, would die for you, because that's the example you've set—you."

Riot stood, thinking on Vet's words and what they meant. The need for alcohol had dulled in the midst of the conversation.

"That's … that's all." Vet really turned to leave this time, still not looking at her.

"Hold up. I'll come with you," Riot said, leaving the glass of whiskey untouched, still in the alcove. "And don't give me too much credit for saving you from that anti-personnel mine. I didn't save your eye."

"It could have been a lot worse." Vet grinned as the two left the mess hall and traveled back through the ship toward the rear cargo bay. "I could have lost a hand or a leg."

"Well then, you could have just been a pirate for Halloween," Riot said, covering the emotion she felt like she always did—with humor. "Hey, I bet we could get a new eye made for you. I mean, you would know better than I would, with the Syndicate tech we have. Would that be possible?"

Vet shrugged, rubbing his steel eye patch with his left hand. "I don't know. I've kind of grown used to this thing. I like pirates."

Riot couldn't help laughing out loud as they exited the ship to join the rest of the unit. Her laugh died on her lips, however, as she saw the worry in their eyes.

14

R iot turned to follow their gaze. The fight in the sky was still taking place between Ketrick and the Scarabs, but the Karnayers were pushing a new frontal assault, not on the dragons or on the city, but offloading ground troops via their bulky transport ships.

The city lay behind Riot and her unit to the north, while the aerial combat took place to the south, and an armada of Karnayer transports were still making their way to the east. There was no way of knowing how many troops they were going to land on the ground, but by the size of the crafts, it looked like thousands.

The Karnayer transport ships weren't as bloated as the ones they had taken down on the Zenoth planet of Raydon, though they were still massive, each as large as the *Valkyrie* with extra room in the cargo section to hold Karnayer soldiers or whatever other alien species they had bent to do their bidding.

We've got to make it to the city before the ground troops do, Rizzo signed. *We'll be caught out here if we don't.*

"I agree with my brother from another mother." Wang turned his helmeted head to Riot. "We're going to have to hump it to make it to the city in time."

"Let's do it," Riot said, hating that the only thing to be done at the moment was running instead of fighting. "I'll take point. Vet, you and Rizzo bring up the rear, with Doctor Miller attached to Wang's hip."

"May I take point with you?" Evonne asked, her white-and-grey uniform streaked with smoke and torn in a dozen places. The skin on her face was still peeled back, showing the metal underneath. She tried to smile, but it just looked like something from a nightmare about to chew Riot's face. The manic blinking she did wasn't helping, either.

"Yes, okay," Riot said, irritated, as she placed her own helmet onto her head. She gripped her weapon and began a light jog down the lane of battered soil the *Valkyrie* had created as it slid to a stop in the jungle. "We really have to work on that blinking thing."

"What? Am I doing it wrong?" Evonne asked as she kept pace with Riot. "Please let me know if I should be blinking a different way."

"You're blinking way too much. No one does that unless they have lint in their contacts," Riot grunted as she kept her eyes open and ears alert. "Blink, like, once every ten or twenty seconds."

"I'll set an internal timer to do so," Evonne said.

"Good," Riot said as she ended the conversation and increased her pace. Her heads-up display was showing the distance of the Savage Trilord city still nine miles from their current location.

Riot took a look behind her and to her right to try to get a reading on how far back the Karnayer transport ships were landing. Her heads-up display rolled though information on a narrow column to her right. It said the transport ships were landing only two miles behind them.

Riot turned back to keeping a steady pace and sweeping the jungle in front of them for any threats. Hypothetically, they should have a clear shot back to the Trilord city, but tombstones were built on hypothetical situations.

"Cardio," Doctor Miller breathed hard from the middle of the pack. "Why does there always have to be so much cardio?"

"Welcome to the Marines," Wang said beside her. "I can't remember a day we didn't have some kind of run involved."

Evonne stopped in her tracks, and Wang and Doctor Miller nearly ran into her.

"Let's go, Sparky," Riot said, also coming to a halt. She didn't try to hide her annoyance. "Clock is ticking."

Evonne stood still as though frozen in time, a very serious expression on her face.

"What's going on?" Vet asked, arriving with Rizzo by his side.

"I don't know," Riot said with a shrug. "Your terminator just decided to stop in the middle of the run and take a breather."

"We should run now," Evonne said in a hard tone Riot had never heard from the AI before. "They're coming quickly."

"Who's coming?" Riot asked, looking behind them at the shell of the *Valkyrie*. "The transport ships are still a few miles behind us."

"The Karnayer troops are not the ones who will be able to catch up to us," Evonne said quickly. "They have brought a species of apex predators capable of running great distances at high speeds. These creatures will catch us before we reach the safety of the city walls."

GREAT, Rizzo wrote across everyone's screens.

Riot stayed still for a moment longer before realizing Evonne had no reason to lie, and she had never been wrong in the past.

"Let's go!" Riot motioned for everyone in the unit to go ahead of her. "Double time. I'm bringing up the rear. Vet, Rizzo, set a strong pace. Evonne, you keep talking. I want to hear how you know this and what we're going to be dealing with. Move!"

At once, everyone began to run. A panicked calm was in the air only hardened soldiers could comprehend. They understood both the urgency of the situation and that they needed to rely on their training.

Riot pumped her legs as the unit ran forward. She chanced another look behind them. To her right, a shadow in the morning light caught her line of sight through the jungle foliage. Was it a shadow, or was her mind playing tricks on her now that she suspected they were being tracked?

Riot couldn't be sure, but whatever she may have seen was gone now. Nothing showed on her heads-up display. It would have been impossible for anything to cover a stretch of two miles so quickly anyway. Riot directed her attention forward, focusing on the run as she listened to Evonne relay all of the information she had on the topic.

"As you all know, the Karnayers have traveled from planet to planet, weaponizing the fiercest warriors and creatures on each world they have visited," Evonne said as she ran with the rest of the unit. Her voice never sounded exhausted despite the pace she was moving. She spoke as if sitting at a dining room table. "It seems they have offloaded a pack of apex predators called Osylots from their transport. These animals would be most similar to a cross between a tiger and a cheetah on your planet."

"How do you know all of this?" Wang asked from his place in the middle of the group. "Are you guessing, or have you seen them?"

"I am still connected with the *Valkyrie*, and as such, I

am able to tap into the ship's long-range sensors. They have picked up the approach of the Osylots."

"How many?" Riot said, concentrating on her breathing. She didn't mind cardio, but she hated having these full-on conversations while she ran. She never understood how people were capable of running while still talking about their frappuccinos that morning. "How many Osylots do you see?"

Evonne ran quiet for a moment. A look of concentration passed through her eyes. "The sensors on the *Valkyrie* have picked up ten signatures, but there may be more. The Osylots possess a keen trait that allows their skin to meld with the colors of their surroundings."

"Awesome," Vet huffed from his spot in the front. "Hunted by camouflaged aliens. This is great."

"Save your breath for running," Riot gasped. Although their armor was made of lightweight material, running in the muggy heat of the jungle was far from easy. Riot's cooling system worked overtime to keep the temperature even.

Soon, the Marines had reached the end of the dirt lane they had used to run, the one the downed *Valkyrie* had cleared for them through the dense jungle. Vet took the lead as the group was forced to run single file.

Strange birds chirped their alien cries. Something that looked like a monkey with massive, round eyes and a small, furry body gawked at them from a tree limb.

Look, Rizzo typed on his forearm as he ran. **It's Wang's last girlfriend**.

Riot couldn't help chuckling, and Vet's laugh also sounded in her helmet.

"Helen was a beautiful woman!" Wang's voice was on the verge of frustration. "How many times do we have to go over this? It's part of their culture; they don't shave."

"Helen had a mustache, dude," Vet said.

"Helen was a beautiful woman," Wang growled through the comms.

Riot could picture her friend's face right now, and the image made her laugh again, despite the stitch in her side. The idea of stopping for a break crossed her mind, but as soon as the thought had appeared, she pushed it down again.

Riot ran at the back of her pack, searching the area behind them as often as she dared. The footing on the jungle floor was tricky, and more than once, she nearly fell as she scanned the closed-in jungle behind her. Every time she looked over her shoulder, her imagination would play tricks on her.

Bushes would move despite the lack of breeze, or the sound of something moving through the jungle opposite them would catch her attention. But each time, nothing showed on her heads-up display.

They ran like this for another half-hour, the sounds of the battle still taking place overhead between the dragons and the Scarabs becoming fainter and fainter the farther they traveled.

"I can't ... I can't run anymore," Doctor Miller gasped as she came to a stop. Hands on her knees, she bent over double. "Just ... just a minute."

"Evonne, how much longer to the city?" Riot studied the area behind her, getting the familiar feeling of being watched.

"Just under a mile," Evonne informed her. "If it weren't for the dense jungle canopy, we'd be able to see the city right now."

"They're out there," Riot said more to herself than anyone in her unit. "I can feel them."

"How come they aren't showing up on our heads-up displays, then?" Wang asked as he passed a canteen to Doctor Miller, who took off her helmet and accepted the water gratefully. "What are they waiting for?"

"If they are cold-blooded creatures, they may not appear in the heads-up display. If they are moving in the jungle around us, there would be no way for the technology to track movements it cannot see," Evonne explained.

"Oh, they're here," Vet said, backing up to where the rest of the unit stood in a circle. "You're right Riot. My spider sense is tingling."

"Your what?" Doctor Miller rose and placed her helmet back on her head.

"It's an old movie reference. I guess a comic book

before that, or something," Vet said, peering down the sight of his Destroyer T9. "It's about a bug boy."

"They were waiting for us to stop." Riot clenched her jaw, readying her weary body for another fight. She peered into the jungle depths, knowing the alien predators were out there, but still not seeing anything. "We hold this point to fend off their initial attack, then move toward the city in a box formation. Vet in the lead, Wang on the right, Rizzo on the left, and myself in the rear. Evonne, you and Doctor Miller in the center."

Everyone moved into position.

Something rushed through the jungle on their left. A twig snapped to their right.

"Here we go again!" Riot roared over the comms. "It's time to go to work."

"Oohrah!" her Marines answered back.

Then the monsters came.

15

In seconds, it was as if the jungle had come alive to kill them.

Creatures painted in the same green-and-purple of the jungle trees and bushes leaped out at them from all sides. Evonne was right in her description of the Osylots. They were large, feline-like creatures with short hair, just bigger than cheetahs. They ran on all fours, but if they stood on their back legs, they would be as tall as humans.

Their multicolored tails were long and swung wildly behind them. One of the most chilling features about the monsters was that even when they attacked, they remained quiet.

Riot and her Marines, on the other hand, made enough noise for the combatants on either side of the conflict.

BOOM! BOOM! BOOM! BOOM!

The War Wolves lit the jungle up with red blaster fire coming from their Villain Pulse Rifles, as well as the Destroyer T9 like shotguns Vet and Rizzo fired. Along with the sounds of discharging weapons came the crashing trees around them as rogue shots cracked trees and lit brush on fire.

In a fight that was taking place so close, Riot had to rely on her reflexes more so than her marksmanship. The Osylots were jumping from the brush on either side of them. Riot shot one of the creatures in the chest, one that would have crashed down onto her had she missed, and another in the face as it swiped at her legs with claws as sharp as knives.

A particularly large Osylot came at Wang from the side and bulldozed into him. A moment later, Wang's red armor was completely covered by the creature's bulk. Its chameleon-like shifting colors made it a beautiful and deadly sight all at once.

Before any of the Marines could move to help Wang, Evonne grabbed the creature with her bare hands, lifted it up over her head, and hurled it back into the jungle.

We should have given this chick a body a lot sooner, Riot thought.

With that show of strength, the oncoming Osylot attack paused for a moment. Bodies from more than a dozen feline creatures smoked at their feet. Riot could only imagine the smell they let off. If not for their helmets cycling clean air, Doctor Miller and Wang would probably be vomiting again.

"You all right?" Riot leaned down and helped Wang to his feet. "Did it puncture your armor?"

"I … I think I'm okay." Wang looked down at himself, checking his legs and arms.

"Rizzo," Doctor Miller said in a panicked voice. "Your face!"

Riot turned her attention to her pilot. One of the Osylots had gotten close enough to the Marine to swipe a claw against the left side of his helmet. Long scratches had etched their way into the metal, but as far as Riot could tell, had not punctured the helmet's dome.

I'm good to go, Rizzo typed into the keyboard on the back of his left forearm.

"Let's move before they regroup and come at us again," Riot said. Her thoughts were already on the rest of the drop ships the Karnayers had flown to the planet. There could be hundreds, maybe thousands, of enemies in the jungle by now.

It was also possible the Osylots had been sent ahead to slow them down long enough for Karnayer soldiers to reach them.

Riot and her team traveled through the jungle in the box formation. All their senses were on overdrive as they swept the jungle for any signs of the enemies they knew to be there. But whether they had killed most of the Osylots or the alien felines had been called back, they did not attack again.

With another ten minutes of jogging, the Marines made it to the main road leading to the capital city of the Savage Trilords. The Trilords at the gate leveled blasters at them when they emerged from the jungle foliage.

"Hold your fire," Queen Revna's familiar voice ordered from the top of the wall. Despite her age, her voice carried the strength any general would envy. "It's our allies. Open the gates!"

Riot was shocked to see the queen, Ketrick's mother, out of the capitol while her city was under attack. She wore steel-and-leather armor over her dark skin. Her long, white hair was put into dreadlocks behind her head. She carried a thick staff with a blaster affixed to the top end.

The colossal double doors to the city opened as Riot and her Marines finally reached the supposed safety of the gates.

The queen traveled down from the top of the wall to embrace Riot.

Riot removed her helmet, extending her right hand to the queen. Revna brushed it aside and wrapped Riot into a hug. Growing up without a mother had made Riot more than awkward around elderly members of her same sex, especially when it came to hugs.

"It is so good to see you again, and safe," Revna said as she pressed Riot harder. "One day you will understand what it is like to see young warriors return safely from combat."

"Uh, yeah—" Riot raised her right hand around Revna's large back and gave her a few quick taps with her palm. "It's good to see you, too."

Revna finally removed herself from the embrace. If she noticed Riot's awkwardness around the hug, she didn't show it.

"You all fought like a hundred in the sky," Revna said to the rest of the Marines under Riot's command. "You must be tired and hungry. Come with me."

Revna moved swiftly through the city and up the hill where the capitol building stood. Two guards, with dragon tattoos marking them as the queen's personal guard, moved with her.

"Should you be out here right now?" Riot said, taking a look at the signs of destruction around the city. "I mean, you need to stay safe in order to lead."

"Would you hide from a fight?" The queen's eyes sparkled with stores of wisdom. "Leaders lead from the front, Riot, you know that."

Riot nodded along with the queen's words. Despite her feelings to want to keep the queen safe, she understood exactly what Revna was talking about. Riot would never ask her crew to do something she wasn't willing to do herself. As the queen of the Savage Trilords, Revna had the same philosophy, only on a much grander scale.

Despite their efforts to keep the city safe, bombed-out buildings dotted the town, along with rubble strewn on the ground. Smoke from fires only recently extinguished dotted the city. Trilord warriors moved tirelessly to make sure any warm embers had been completely put out.

From what Riot could see, a good quarter of the town had been razed. This fact hadn't seemed to faze the queen. She walked boldly back to the pyramid that stood on the top of the hill, speaking words of encouragement to those she passed. What's more, she seemed to know all of her warriors by name.

"Get some rest, Sloan," Revna said to a muscular, shaven-head Trilord who carried buckets of water in each of his hands down the city hill. "You've been at it all night."

The Trilord bowed his head to his queen.

"Noe," Revna said to another tall Trilord carting a load of weapons to the front gate. "Eat something, even if it's a duckhole, before you fall down. That's not a request."

"Yes, my queen." The Trilord nodded and continued on his way.

"The Trilords will run themselves into the ground before they stop fighting," Revna said to Riot. "As I'm sure you would, as well."

Riot blinked, trying to keep them open even as the queen made her statement.

"We'll do what needs to be done to be the last one standing," Riot said, looking past the city to her left where Ketrick still battled with the ships, keeping the Scarabs at bay. "Your son is holding them back, but they have troops in the jungle now. We need to be prepared for a ground assault at any moment."

"Oh, I think we can expect a break in the fighting soon," Revna said as they reached the top of the hill and the pyramid that stood sentry. The square stone pyramid separated in layers was battered and scorched.

More than a handful of pockmarks showered where the Scarabs had landed shots, and though the stone was strong enough to hold up against most of the fire, there was a spot on the south side about halfway up that had crumbled. A small crater stood out. Another spot near the top where Rippa's mech unit stood showed signs of damage.

As they got closer, Rippa's mech unit began to slide down the pyramid side, level by level.

Then, something Revna had said caught Riot's attention. "Why do you think there will be a break in the fighting soon?"

"Because our allies have arrived," Revna said in the matter-of-fact, faithful way Riot had heard Ketrick speak so many times before. "You, my son, every warrior human, Trilord, or other has done enough to stay the hand of destruction."

Riot squinted through the bright morning light to try to catch any sign of the approaching Grovothe ships. There were no large vessels on the horizon, only the swooping, swirling fighting going on between the dragons and the Scarab ships.

Riot was about to open her mouth, when Rippa made the final descent down the pyramid wall in her mech. The ground shuddered as the machine came to a halt in front of them.

Unlike the pyramid, Rippa's mech had not fared so well. The dark armor on her mech was dented, and sparks burst out of a spot around where the left leg of the mech connected to the rest of the body. The torso was caved in and the right arm of the unit looked like it was attached by only a few hoses.

The unit opened with a hiss. The pilot seat was stationed in the torso. As the hatch opened, a slender ladder rolled down. The red-haired Grovothe wasted no time in dismounting as she talked wildly.

"Riot, everyone, you guys made it!" Rippa jumped the last few feet to the floor. Bags hung under her eyes, but the fire of war shone bright. "I was just about to get you over the comms. They're here. Admiral Tricon and the *Dreadnaught* are entering orbit. We did it!"

Riot couldn't help her mouth falling open as she turned to Revna. The queen gave her a small smile and a wink.

"Look," Vet said, shading his own good eye as he searched the skyline. "There, to the south, just past where the dragons are still fighting."

All eyes followed Vet's gaze as they, too, searched

for the sign of hope they had so desperately been fighting to see.

Riot shaded her own view as her tired eyes fought the bright light of the twin Hoydren suns and tried to see what Vet was talking about. Then, like a steel angel descending from the heavens, the *Dreadnaught* started as a tiny black pinpoint. With each second, it grew in size, until the large ship was visible. Its steep lines and sheer bulk made it look just as intimidating as any Karnayer class destroyer.

The Scarab ships swirling around the dragons thought better of their position and retreated to the east, where the transport ships also lifted off the jungle floor and departed.

"Where's Alveric and the Trilord destroyer we saw earlier?" Doctor Miller asked, a question everyone was thinking. "Why didn't they try to intercept the *Dreadnaught?*"

There was a brief moment of silence before the queen answered.

"They have their troops on the ground now. This has all been a distraction to get their ground forces in a position to strike," Revna said with steel in her voice. "One way or another, the next battle will be the last."

16

The food that was sent to Riot's room while she bathed tasted better than anything she had ever stuffed into her mouth before. Maybe it was the fact she was so hungry, or the idea that she was still alive and able to enjoy the food. Either way, the meat tasted glorious, and the warm bread stuff, like manna from Heaven.

Sleep was going to have to wait. Thanks to the temporary lapse in attacks by the Karnayers, Riot and the rest of the alliance had an opportunity to catch their breath. The idea now was for a strategy meeting to be held.

With Admiral Tricon landing his forces on Hoydren and Ketrick pulling his dragons back, a new plan of attack needed to be discussed. It was decided a war council would be held in the pyramid palace building in thirty minutes. That gave Riot thirty minutes to wash herself and feed her face.

Showers didn't seem to be an option, but luxurious baths, on the other hand, were readily available. Riot soaked in the warm, ceramic tub, trying to ignore what was on her body. When she stripped off her armor, purple flakes of gore from the Devil's Hand had come off with it. That, along with the smoke smell and her own sweat, had been enough for Riot to want to burn the armor. But she would need to don her gear at least one more time before all of this was over.

The room she sat in was one of the chambers facing the outside of the pyramid. In front of her, a slanted wall with a window showed a view of the open jungle spreading out to the south and east.

Next to her was a tray of food, and one with cleaning supplies like soap, something that looked like a long sponge, and three seashells Riot had no idea how to use.

Soon, the hot, clear water turned soapy and then to a grimy color as the filth left her body and was washed into the bathwater.

I just need an hour of sleep, Riot's muddled mind thought as she was enticed to slumber by the warm water. *Just an hour of sleep.*

Riot's eyes were closing of their own accord, when a harsh knock echoed into her room.

"I'm awake, I'm awake!" Riot's eyes snapped open as

she forgot where she was for a moment and jolted upright in the bath. "Who is it?"

"Only a lowly prince come to see the mighty warrior who stayed the main force of the Karnayer horde," Ketrick's voice echoed through the door. "I brought you some clean clothes, and I'm going to take your armor to be washed and repaired."

"Just a minute," Riot said, standing from her bath, grabbing a towel, and drying herself off. She was in the middle of wondering how Ketrick was so energetic when the answer struck her. "Ketrick, have you been drinking more coffee?"

"Can I come in?" Ketrick asked from the opposite side of the door.

"Yes." Riot stepped out of the tub and wrapped the towel around her damp body.

Ketrick opened the door. It was clear that he had not taken the time to bathe. He stepped into the room still wearing the same gear he had charged the Devil's Hand with. Black smoke marks smeared his face, slimy blue guck clinging to him. In his right hand, he carried a clean uniform, and in his left, a tall cup of steaming coffee.

"Colonel Harlan managed to land his craft, and his mess hall is still working." Ketrick handed Riot the Marine uniform he had also taken from the ship. "Why didn't you tell me there were so many kinds of coffee? Espresso, cappuccino, cocaine."

"Hold on, take it easy there," Riot said, accepting the

clothes with a shake of her head. "Cocaine is not a kind of coffee. Where did you even learn that word?"

"Brother Wang was talking about it like it was something to be used to stay awake," Ketrick said with a shrug as Riot took another gulp of his coffee. "Anyway, I'm glad you made it back safely."

"Yeah, you, too," Riot said, exhaling. Feelings like she had never felt before were causing her to say words she had never said before. Instead of being sappy, though, she redirected the conversation. "How did you get the dragons to come help you? Were any injured when you fought the Scarabs?"

"The dragons, as you call them, love this planet just as much as we do. When they understood the threat, they agreed to send their best warriors to help. Vikta also played a large part in convincing them," Ketrick said, grabbing Riot's armor with his free hand. He lifted the gear like it was a toy. "We lost two today. Their hides are near impenetrable, but their eyes and certain parts of their wings where their skin is the thinnest are susceptible to injury."

Riot noticed the downcast eyes, the slump in Ketrick's shoulders as he said these words. For the first time, she saw past the false caffeinated front he was putting on and realized how weary he really was.

Riot went to him and lifted his face with her right hand so he would look into her eyes.

"They died protecting something they believed in, like you or I are willing to do, as well," Riot said with a small smile. "They died a warrior's death so we could live, maybe to one day do the same for others."

"Careful." Ketrick smiled his fangy grin. "You're starting to sound like me."

"I know," Riot laughed, dropping her hand from his face. "I realized that while the words were coming out of my mouth. Who am I?"

"I'm going to give you a hug," Ketrick said, and before Riot could move, the Trilord wrapped his massive, dirty, sweaty arms around her.

"I just took a bath!" Riot screamed and laughed at the same time. "I don't even want to move. I'm just going to get even dirtier. What's with you and your family giving hugs, anyway?"

Ketrick released her a moment later, a smile cracking his own lips. He took another long swig of the coffee. "Listen, I know we talked about waiting, but after the meeting, I'd like to take you out on our first official romantic getaway."

"Ketrick, we're in a war zone," Riot said, stealing the coffee mug from his hand and downing a long swig of the hot liquid. "And we're going on our second day of no sleep."

"Tomorrow may be too late." Ketrick walked to the door and looked back with a smile. "Let's make the most of this lull in the battle."

"All right"—Riot took another gulp of coffee—"but something quick. We're going to need to sleep if we're going to face the Karnayer forces."

"Agreed, Sorceress," Ketrick said, closing the door behind him.

Riot busied herself getting ready. Her weary hands buttoned her uniform while she guzzled the strong coffee in between preparing for the meeting. When she exited her room a few minutes later, Killa was coming down the hall to collect her.

"You look tired," Killa said to Riot with a worried sideways glance.

"Thanks, thanks for that." Riot rubbed at her eyes. "It's because I am. We fought through the night. Has there been any word on Karnayer movement since they landed?"

"None," Killa said, motioning for Riot to follow her down the halls of the Trilord pyramid. "It would worry me, but there can only be one logical explanation."

"And that would be?" Riot asked trying to keep pace with the long-legged female general.

Killa led Riot to the end of the hall and down a series of stairs to the main floor. Her silence was strange. Riot knew she had heard her question and it wasn't like the Trilord to be rude.

Finally, she answered. Her voice was full of worry. "They're waiting for something. The only thing that it could be is for the remaining forces from Earth to arrive."

"Wait, that doesn't make any sense," Riot said, thinking out the strategy behind her scrunched brow.

"Wouldn't they want to attack now while our forces are divided. Unless..."

Riot and Killa stopped by a set of tall doors leading into a side chamber. Killa turned to Riot, nodding. "Keep talking. You're right in what you suspect."

"Unless they are so sure of victory, they want to kill us all at once. They don't want to be engaged with us on this front, only to have General Armon drop out of hyperspace and attack them from the rear," Riot said out loud, although at this point, she was speaking more to herself than to the Trilord leader. "Alveric's one cocky son of a gun."

"There may be more to his plan, but I suspect you are correct in your assumption." Killa placed a large hand on the door handle and swung the door open. "After you."

Riot entered the room where Queen Revna, Colonel Harlan, and Admiral Tricon stood talking on the other side of the chamber. As far as the rooms in the pyramid went, this was more of a mid-sized boardroom. On the bottom level, it was located somewhere on the left side of the pyramid. Long windows along the left wall allowed late morning light to splay inside the room. The area was bare, with only a few chairs wreathing a long, oval table.

Queen Revna turned with a smile. "You're right on time. My son, on the other hand, is late. He should be arriving soon, shouldn't he?"

"I, uh, I mean, why would you ask me? How would I

know?" Riot said, the words tumbling out of her mouth like a high school-aged student caught playing hooky. "I was bathing and dressing in my room."

The queen gave Riot a look that said, *I know exactly what happened, but let's move on.*

"Good to see you whole," Colonel Harlan said from his spot next to the Grovothe admiral. He and Riot traded salutes. "When I saw the *Valkyrie* go down, my first instinct was to go after you. The thrusters in the *Titan* were gone, though. We were barely staying off the ground."

"I understand," Riot said, joining the group, with Killa at her side. "We made it back in one piece."

Riot turned to salute Admiral Tricon next. The shorter, bearded Grovothe looked dashing as always in his pristine uniform. He replied with a salute of his own.

"Thank you for coming," Riot said to the newest member of their alliance. "I know the Trilords aren't technically approved allies of the Grovothe yet. You could have stood down if you wanted to and just looked the other way."

"Others may have." Admiral Tricon nodded along with Riot's words. "But we share a common enemy, and we are stronger united. I have it on good authority that the Trilords will be listed as our allies soon. It took a small act from the Allfather to get Earth acknowledged as allies so quickly. I suspect more than a few on our homeworld see the wisdom in a united front."

The doors to the meeting room banged open, and Ketrick ran in. His long, black hair was still wet. He wore the traditional Trilord clothing of long pants and boots, greaves, and no shirt.

If there had ever been a gathering of more different beings in the universe, Riot would love to see them.

"Admiral, Colonel, Mother," Ketrick said to the heads of the alliance before turning to Killa and Riot with a grin.

"Good to see you once more," Admiral Tricon cracked through a thin smile. "I just arrived and have already heard about your winged attack on the Karnayer Scarabs. That took courage."

"Thank you, Admiral," Ketrick returned the nod. His smile soon faded into a frown. "It had to be done. Two winged brothers gave their lives to buy us the time we needed."

"I understand." The admiral sighed heavily. "I'm afraid victory against Alveric and the rogue House of Karn will entail more sacrifice from all of us."

The room grew quiet as everyone took a moment to consider how true the admiral's words really were.

"Shall we begin?" Queen Revna motioned for the group to gather around the oval table in the center of the room. "It's time to plan the greatest war this planet has ever seen."

17

"My mech squads should take front positions on the walls when they come." Admiral Tricon looked down at the table where Killa had spread a cream-colored map. "I'll leave them here under Major Rippa's command and take the fight to the Karnayer destroyer orbiting the planet."

Riot's eyes raced over the map, tracking the admiral's words along with what she was seeing in front of her. The Trilord capital was on a hill with the dense jungle extending to the south and west. To the east was flat, then rolling lands that led to the Brute faction, while the north extended miles through rough terrain before a massive mountain range marked the end of the map.

"I wish I could join you, but the *Titan* is out of the fight." Colonel Harlan looked down at the map, shaking his head. "The *Valkyrie* is out, as well. Until General Armon gets here with our space force from Earth, you and Ketrick's dragons are our only weapons in the sky."

"We'll hold them until your general arrives." Admiral Tricon stroked his grey beard. "We'll play defense until then. Once the force from Earth arrives, we can concentrate on blowing that destroyer out of the air."

"We have a great chance of ending the Karnayers here." Ketrick crossed his arms over his massive chest. "We can't let them escape."

While the others were discussing the placement of troops and strategy, memories of the conversation Riot had just had with Killa played back in her mind. She looked over to the Trilord commander, and the two shared a troubled glance.

"We should anticipate we're doing everything they want us to do," Riot said, bringing all eyes around the table up to her. "They have creatures fighting for them from every corner of the universe. Creatures they've captured and bent to their will. We've come up against a few of them already. Who knows what Alveric unloaded in the jungle?"

"You think he wanted all of this to happen?" Queen Revna asked.

"It would seem that he wants us all here together, humans included, in order to kill us in one fell swoop,"

Commander Killa said, nodding to Riot. "We should be prepared for anything."

A moment of silence passed over the room as each of the minds in the chamber thought on Riot's and Killa's words.

"Admiral Tricon has the most experience of fighting the Karnayers, and the tactics the Karnayers use," Queen Revna said, looking over to the shorter Grovothe. "I'm willing to have you take the lead on this conflict."

"Thank you," Admiral Tricon said as he looked over at the others around the table. "We keep the plan simple and play defense until the rest of the force from Earth arrives. Then we reassess. If the Karnayers have still not attacked, then we take the fight to them, with myself and General Armon attacking through the air. The Trilords and my mech units will take the ground forces through the jungle. I can even afford to send some Grovothe shock troops with you, as well."

"The War Wolves aren't going to sit by," Riot said, looking over to Colonel Harlan. "I don't think any Marine plans on doing that."

"You bet your ass." Colonel Harlan grinned at Riot. "If and when it comes down to an attack, we'll be there, leading the charge. Tip of the spear."

"Then it's decided." Ketrick rubbed at his weary eyes. Naturally red, it was hard to tell how tired he really was. "Defense, until it is time to go on the offensive."

"Let's get what rest we can," Queen Revna said, dismissing the room. "I think the next time we have a lull in the fight, we'll either be the victors or have much larger issues to deal with."

The room emptied, with Admiral Tricon talking with Colonel Harlan about troop strength and what forces General Armon would be bringing with him. Killa and Queen Revna stayed behind in the room, talking in low tones about their own troops and placement of the city defenses.

But fatigue was muddling Riot's thought process. She knew she should be thinking of a hundred other things at the moment, but right now, only three things could occupy her mind: the state of her team, sleep, and the mischievous grin Ketrick had plastered across his face.

"Before you pass into a sleeping coma"—Ketrick motioned for Riot to follow him—"I have something to show you."

"Will do." Riot stifled a yawn and rubbed at her eyes. "Sorry, I'm still up for our date. Let me just check in on the rest of the squad. I'll follow you."

Ketrick nodded along with Riot's words as he led her through the pyramid and to a stairwell located in the corner of the structure. The pyramid was empty for the most part, with servants turned into soldiers and more than likely guarding the walls or preparing for another attack.

"Evonne, can you patch me through to Vet?" Riot

asked the AI via the nanites that connected her to everyone else.

"Right away," Evonne responded at once. "You are now connected."

"Thanks," Riot huffed as she followed Ketrick up multiple flights of stairs. Trying to keep pace with the Trilord prince was nearly impossible. Wherever he was going, he was excited to get there. "Vet, can you hear me?"

"But I want to wear the pretty dress tonight," Vet responded in a mumbled tone.

Riot scrunched her brow, trying to figure out what was happening. "Vet? Vet, can you hear me?"

"You promised I could be the ballerina tonight."

"Vet, wake up!" Riot said, finally understanding what she was listening to. "You can be the ballerina when we get back to Earth. Today you're a Marine!"

"What! Who? Riot?"

"Vet, pull yourself together, man," Riot said, holding in a chuckle. "What's your status?"

"Oh, right, sorry," Vet said with a yawn. "Rizzo, Wang, and I are bunked up. Doc wanted to get a few reports in. Evonne is taking care of repairs on our armor and weapons. Rippa went to speak with the admiral and make repairs on her mech."

"Roger that," Riot said, nearly tripping on another step. She looked down at the army of switchback stairs she had just climbed. She was about halfway to the top of the pyramid. "Get as much sleep and food in you as you can handle. One way or another, this fight is going to end soon. We're on notice to get back into the action when the Karnayers attack, and if they don't, we'll be mounting our own offense when General Armon and the rest of the fleet arrive."

"Copy," Vet said over the nanites. "We'll be ready to roll when the time comes."

"I know you will," Riot said. "Now get back to your dreams of being a ballerina."

"What?" Vet sounded half-panicked, half-ignorant to what she was talking about. "I don't want to be a ballerina."

"Hey, man, we all have our secrets," Riot said as Ketrick looked back at her with a wide grin of his own. "I'm not judging you."

"Dance is a highly respected art and takes years of training," Vet said, catching himself close to admitting something. "If … if I wanted to be on Broadway, which I don't."

"Whatever you say, Twinkle Toes." Riot didn't say anything else. There was a silence on the other end, signaling Vet had signed off and was going back to sleep.

Riot's brow was beginning to perspire as she and Ketrick crested the last set of stairs leading to a hatch-like entrance placed into the top of the pyramid.

Ketrick reached up and opened the latch. The final floor of the stairwell was located directly in the middle of the pyramid.

Riot had to look back at how far they had come to understand that the stairwell they climbed actually sent them on a diagonal path from the corner bottom floor of the pyramid to the center top of the structure.

When Ketrick opened the hatch, a brilliant light made Riot wince. She looked at Ketrick through tired eyes, managing to raise an eyebrow in his direction. "Look, Muscles, this is cute and all, but a girl's got to get her sleep if she's going to take on the bulk of the Karnayer army soon."

"Trust me," Ketrick said as he winked. He climbed up the few ladder rungs set into the wall and hoisted himself out of sight.

A moment later, Riot followed, grabbing onto the rungs as she pulled herself to the rooftop. What she saw took her breath away.

Ketrick stood at her side as the two looked out on the Trilord city and the surrounding landscape of Hoydren. They were on the very top of the square pyramid, more than a hundred feet in the air. The square landing pad they stood on was no more than a twenty-by-twenty block of brick. Scorch marks and pockets of debris marked the area like acne on a teenager.

This was the place where Rippa had made her stand inside her mech when the Karnayers made their run on the city.

Twin suns beat down warm rays on Riot, but this

high up, a cool breeze ran past her body and played with her short, dark hair.

While Riot was still taking in the scene Ketrick was busy unpacking a large basket of what looked like pillows and blankets.

"I'm not much of a cuddler," Riot said, moving over to help. "Where did all of this stuff come from, anyway?"

"Perks of being a prince is that you can ask servants to do strange things, like arrange for there to be a canopy and a pile of blankets and pillows on top of the capitol building, and they run to fulfill your request," Ketrick said as he erected a square awning with white metal poles and a blue fabric top. "And you're in luck. I'm not a cuddler, either."

"If we make it out of this thing alive," Riot said, grabbing a handful of blankets and pillows to place under the shade, "you're in trouble."

"*When* we make it out, you mean." Ketrick plopped himself down onto the makeshift sleeping area. "You mean *when* we make it out, and I happen to like trouble."

Riot lowered her guard, something that was becoming slightly easier with practice. She took a spot next to Ketrick, her left shoulder and arm rested against his right. The blankets underneath her and the pillows against her head nearly swaddled her in an embrace of sleep.

"You did good, kid," Riot said to Ketrick as she

placed her hand in his. "I can't remember the last time I held hands with anyone. I feel a little like an awkward teenager right now. Ketrick? Uh, Ketrick?"

Riot looked over to see the Trilord prince fast asleep his mouth wide open and a line of drool rolling out from the corner of his left lip.

Riot couldn't help grinning to herself. She gave his hand a squeeze, then rolled over onto her side. Sleep came for her instantly, a nightmare only a half-step behind.

18

Riot had a feeling there had been more to her dream leading up to this point, but whatever it had been wasn't making itself known. All there was now was a nightmare she had relived over and over and over again since it had taken place in college.

It was the moment that had begun her descent into true alcoholism, the moment that had set her on a course that would lead her into the Marines.

She and the man she thought she loved had been drinking. Through his inebriation, it had come out that he had cheated on her. An argument was about to take place, one where Riot would find herself on the ground, stars bursting across her vision after he'd struck her.

Unlike previous nightmares, Riot was actually herself in this dream. He was standing in front of her, spewing out reasons why she wasn't good enough, calling her names.

It was about to happen.

"Well, I'm done with you," Riot said as her eyes swam with tears. "We're over."

The strike came like it had come a million times before. In her dreams or in her waking memories, it was always the same. A right cross connecting with the left side of her chin. Riot was powerless to do anything to help her former self besides sit in her own body and watch it happen.

She fell backwards, the tang of metallic touching her taste buds as though it were an old friend.

As Riot fell backwards she struck her head on the hard wooden floor of his apartment.

She lay there stunned. She knew what was coming —a thousand apologies and tears from the man she didn't even really know. He would beg her to take him back, blame the strike on an accident, then the alcohol, and then beg some more.

This is where Riot would burst into even more tears. She'd get up and walk out on him forever. These events would haunt her until she'd buried them down deep. She'd focus on drinking and her career as a Marine in the years to come.

But something was different now. This time in her dream, Riot actually had control of her body. A feeling of strength and contentment started in her left shoulder and slowly coursed through her body.

For whatever reason this time, she wasn't doomed to repeat the events, only watching out through her eyes like a caged captive. Riot lifted herself off the ground. She waved his hands away. She spat blood as he continued to apologize and try to gather her in a hug.

"I'm sorry, I'm so sorry, Gertrude," he said with panicked, drunken eyes. "I don't know what happened. We can fix this."

Riot massaged the left side of her face where his clumsy strike had hit her. She was still in awe that she actually had control of her body at this point.

"Gert, are you okay?" He came to her again, trying to touch the area on her split lip where blood still gushed. "I'm so sorry, I'm so sorry."

His right hand reached for her face. Riot grabbed his pointer and middle fingers with her left hand and cranked them to the side so hard she felt his fingers break right before his entire body followed in that direction.

"Ahhh!"

It felt good to hear him scream. In fact, it felt great.

Riot still wasn't sure why this time she had been granted the power to control her body, but she was loving the freedom it brought with it. Tears, not of pain or sorrow, filled her eyes.

"You—you—" He struggled to his feet again, his inebriated state dulling the pain of his broken fingers. A madness crossed through his eyes as he collected himself from the floor and charged. "You made me do this!"

Instead of side-stepping his charge, Riot crouched against his larger frame and leveraged him back a few steps like an offensive lineman. She grabbed both his arms and sent the crown of her head into his nose, once, twice, three times just for good measure.

Crimson red oozed from his broken nose. From both nostrils, the blood splattered everywhere. His pressed suit and tie were soon dyed red by his own bodily fluids. Riot released him as he slumped to his knees, dazed.

"You did this," Riot said, looking down at his swaying form. "This wasn't my fault. This was never my fault. Or maybe it was. Maybe it was on me for letting myself ever give you a chance. Either way, I'm done now. I'm not going to let your memory handicap me for the rest of my life."

"Gert, Gertrude!" He grabbed on to her right hand, unable to rise from his knees. "You'll be back. You're mine. You belong to me."

Riot grabbed his perfectly combed hair and lifted his already blackening eyes to her own. "My name is Riot."

Riot drove her right knee up into the bottom of his chin so hard his head snapped back. He fell to the wooden floor, motionless.

The feeling of happiness and closure that had started in her left shoulder was stronger than ever, and more hot tears splashed down Riot's face. Even in her dream state, she knew something special had just taken place.

Riot woke, lying on her right side. How long the smile had been on her face was impossible to tell. Tears of happiness streaked her chin.

Ketrick's steady breathing was constant behind her. During the course of their nap, he, too, had rolled onto his right side. His left hand had found its way to her shoulder, his large palm placed gently on her.

Riot wiped her eyes and rolled over onto her left side to look at the Trilord Prince. His hand slipped down from her shoulder as she moved. He opened his red eyes, looking into hers.

Sleep still clouded his eyes he gazed at her. "Have you just been watching me while I slumber, Sorceress?"

Ketrick yawned, showing off his long, canine teeth.

"I don't know how that translates on your planet," Ketrick said with a mischievous grin, "but here on Hoydren, that would indicate you care for me. That, or you are plotting to kill me in my sleep."

"I think we'll keep you around a little longer." Riot leaned in and pressed her lips against his. "We need someone to control the dragons when the Karnayers come."

Ketrick moved into a sitting position. "How long have we been asleep?"

Riot moved to sit next to him. She followed his gaze to where Hoydren's twin suns set in the distance, their bright rays just now sinking under the horizon. Noise this high up was almost non-existent. Far down below, Riot could hear the faint voices of guards and soldiers doing their part to prepare for the fight to come.

"General Armon will have arrived by now." Riot stood up, stretching. Memories of her dream came back to her, for once vivid and clear. "We should get down and see what needs to be done. If Alveric and the House of Karn don't attack soon, I imagine we'll be on the offensive shortly."

Ketrick stood beside her, reeling in her gaze from the setting suns that cast a red glow on the sky far above.

"Were you crying? Are you all right?" Ketrick asked with nothing but genuine concern.

"Yeah," Riot said, smiling over at him. "For the first time in a very long time, I can honestly say I'm all right. But one way or another, a fight's coming. It's time to reel in touchy-emotional Riot and bring out the beast. You know what I'm talking about."

"I do," Ketrick said, leaning down and kissing her on the forehead. "Just give me one last moment with my Riot before you lock her away."

Riot felt his warm lips touch her skin. She let herself be vulnerable for a moment longer.

BOOM!

Riot was ripped from the moment of comfort, her eyes darting to where the noise had come from. Far below and to the south of the city, a plume of smoke rose through the dense jungle brush.

BOOM!

The same sound came again, shattering the silence, even at her current altitude. Riot strained harder to see what could be causing it, but just like before, only a plume of dark smoke rose up from the jungle floor.

BOOM!

A third explosion erupted, right next to the first two. A third curl of smoke rose into the darkening sky.

"What are they doing?" Riot asked, straining to see, willing herself to see something in the distance.

"I don't know, but it's not good." Ketrick's eyes were full of worry. "Let's go."

Riot and Ketrick ran down the same stairs they had ascended when climbing to the top of the Trilord pyramid.

The few hours of sleep Riot had taken with Ketrick had been truly amazing. Whether the nanites aided in her body's repair, or maybe her muscles and joints were just grateful to get a handful of hours of sleep, Riot didn't know. Either way, she felt refreshed and ready to enter the fight once more.

Riot tapped into the nanites that acted as her comms as she took stairs two at a time with Ketrick. "Evonne, report. What's going on out there?"

"It seems the Karnayers have begun their assault, or at least the preparation to do so," Evonne answered back in her even, matter-of-fact way of speaking.

"Should I have the rest of the team meet you somewhere with armor and weapons?"

"Yes," Riot said as her mind went down a mental checklist of places to gather her men and change into her armor. "Have them meet me at the entrance to the pyramid. I want to check in with General Armon and Colonel Harlan before I get ahead of myself."

"Understood," Evonne answered. "I'll let them know."

Riot and Ketrick finally reached the bottom floor at a run and raced through the ground level of the pyramid.

The booming in the distance neither grew in volume nor became more rapid; it was just a constant boom that somehow brought a feeling of dread.

Ketrick and Riot almost ran right into Rippa and Admiral Tricon as the two Grovothe headed for the main throne room in the palace. Each of the Grovothe wore a look so serious, Riot didn't even want to ask what they knew.

"I know I'm going to regret this, but—" Riot looked from Rippa to the admiral. "What's out there? What have the Karnayers brought with them now?"

"Abominations," Rippa said, swallowing hard. "They've brought Abominations."

19

"Maybe just lie to me for a second," Riot said, trying to prep herself to hear whatever it was Admiral Tricon and Rippa knew. "Tell me they brought some kind of mutant kittens with them."

Admiral Tricon either didn't understand Riot's humor or was too focused on what he was doing next to joke. "We're heading to Queen Revna's throne room now where General Armon and Colonel Harlan are waiting. The general came in north of the city a few hours ago but insisted we let you and your squad rest. He said we'd need you at your best very soon."

"Good to know," Riot said, falling into step with Admiral Tricon and Rippa as they headed to meet the others. Riot looked over at Rippa with a raised eyebrow. "Abominations, huh? Worse than the Devil's Hand? Who comes up with these names, anyway?"

"I am unsure." Rippa shrugged. "Someone with a lot of time on their hands. But the Abominations are … not like what we have seen before."

"Well, that just makes me feel all warm and tingly inside." Riot sighed. "Just tell me they bleed. If they bleed, we can kill them."

Before Rippa could give Riot an answer, they reached the door leading into the palace room. The massive doors were wide open, giving them a clear view of Queen Revna speaking with General Armon.

The two broke off their conversation as Riot and her party entered. General Armon and Riot traded salutes.

"From everything I've heard, you've done one heck of a job here. I'm sure I'll be reading all about every detail from Doctor Miller soon in a report the size of an encyclopedia," General Armon said to Riot with a nod, his perfect, graying buzz cut intact, and as military as ever. "I didn't want to wake you when we arrived. You and your team deserved the downtime. I wish I could give you more."

"We're ready to roll out whenever you need us, sir." Riot returned the nod to the general. "I think Admiral Tricon and Rippa may have information on the noise coming from the jungle."

All eyes in the room swung over to the two Grovothe. Admiral Tricon traced the scar on the right side of his head, as if by touching the wound, it would bring back memories of the aliens they now faced.

"Alveric is deploying Abominations across the battlefield." Admiral Tricon looked past everyone in the room as if he were seeing, somewhere against the far wall, the events he now explained. "I've only encountered them once before. I didn't think Alveric would have been entrusted with the Karnayer unit. The Abominations are like the Karnayers' ultimate weapon. This is why Alveric wasn't worried about allowing us to gather en masse. He wanted all of us together to unleash the Abominations on us all at once."

"What are they?" Riot asked. "What are the Abominations?"

"Something half-dead, half-machine, brought to life by magic." Admiral Tricon snapped out of his distant memories with a start. "One of them gave me this scar when I was a corporal in the Grovothe shock troop division. We were sent out to investigate a dead planet. There wasn't supposed to be life there. All of a sudden, we were getting pings of energy readings. I was sent in with my division and what we found there were ... monsters, more machine than organic."

"Anything can be killed," General Armon said in a soft but stern tone. "Were there any weak points on these Abominations? Where did they come from? What weapons do they use?"

"They're not an alien species," Admiral Tricon said, back to his normal gruff self. Whatever memories had been dredged up by the mention of the Abominations had been locked down once more. "They were experiments done by the Karnayers on the dead. They melded machine parts to dead beings and somehow brought them back. When we engaged them, they just kept coming. They cut my unit to shreds. They walked through blaster fire like it was nothing more than rain."

"How did you get out?" Queen Revna asked.

"We called for heavy artillery drops once we evacuated the war zone." Admiral Tricon cleared his throat. "We lost more than half the unit for nothing. Archangel transports picked us up, and we sent orbital strikes covering the entire area. When we went back in, they were gone. There was nothing left—no body parts, no machine parts; they just disappeared. We told ourselves we had destroyed them in the orbital strikes, but I think everyone who was there had an idea that they could have escaped."

"Air support will be difficult," General Armon said, looking at everyone in the room. "They'll know that we'll counter against these Abominations with strikes from the sky. Alveric will move against us with his fleet as soon as we take to the air. He doesn't even have to beat us in the sky; he just has to keep us busy enough to allow his ground forces to overrun the city."

"With respect, sir," Rippa said, turning to the admiral. "I've never met an enemy that could stand up against a squad of mech warriors. Let me lead the mechs we have left and stand with the city."

"Not even a question." Admiral Tricon's eyes shone with fire. "Don't mistake my memories for defeat.

We're going to give the House of Karn a fight. My resolve has not changed. Rippa leads the mechs, as well as a ground contingent of Grovothe shock troops."

"We'll see how we fare against the Abominations." General Armon looked to Queen Revna and Admiral Tricon for consent. "If we're in danger of being overrun, then we take to the sky and fight it out there."

"Alveric will be doing the same," Ketrick said from his spot beside Riot. "He'll hold his fleet in check, waiting to counter our move if we try to perform bombing runs on his ground troops."

"We have the intel Admiral Tricon has given us about the Abominations, but we should have eyes on the targets as soon as possible to monitor their movement," Riot said. "Let me take the War Wolves out into the jungle and get eyes on target. We'll be better equipped to defend against them if we know their exact force size and movements."

Ketrick opened his mouth like he was about to protest, but was silenced with a stern stare from Riot.

"Agreed." General Armon looked to the queen and the admiral to make sure there was no opposition to the plan. When they nodded, he continued. "Take your crew into the jungle and report back. We'll stay here and prepare to defend the city."

"Roger that," Riot said, saluting, and turned to leave the room. Ketrick and Rippa fell in stride beside her.

"I'm not letting you go alone," Ketrick said in a

hurried whisper. "This could be a trap. Alveric has to know we'd send a force out to gather intel."

"For once I agree with the oversized child-man." Rippa had to lightly jog to keep up with the other two. "This is a dangerous plan."

"Listen," Riot said, traveling through the doors of the room and heading for the entrance to the pyramid where her gear and unit would be waiting. "I'm not asking you two to come. My unit is more than capable of lying on our bellies and viewing the enemy through a pair of binoculars. We can handle this."

"I need to go grab my weapons," Rippa said, ignoring Riot's words. "I can meet you in a few minutes. Don't leave without me."

"As do I," Ketrick said without pausing for Riot to respond. "I'll be back before Rippa. Her tiny, child-like legs do not accommodate fast travel."

The Grovothe and Trilord went off in opposite directions before Riot could reply. A part of her was grateful to be surrounded by friends unwilling to allow her to brave the threat of the jungle at night. On the other hand, she wished they would let her go by herself. There was no need to put everyone in danger. If it were an option at all, she would have volunteered to go take a look at the Abominations herself, leaving her unit behind, but she knew General Armon would never go for that.

Riot reached the entrance to the pyramid as the last light of day died to the coming darkness. A million and one stars twinkled overhead in the clear sky. The giant moon that reigned over Hoydren's night seemed brighter than ever.

So, what's the word? Rizzo signed. *Let me guess: We're going to go see what that ominous booming sound in the jungle is.*

"You're smarter than you look." Riot grinned, looking at her men and Evonne, who stood next to them carrying Riot's armor and weapons. "You all geared up and ready to go?"

"Good to go," Vet said, dusting off the shoulder of his own armor. "What's the plan?"

Riot chose a place to change just inside the pyramid entrance, where the alcove would protect her from two sides. She immediately went to work undressing to her underwear and accepting the armor Evonne handed to her. The AI stood right in front of her, blocking her from any prying eyes.

Vet, Wang, and Rizzo turned their backs while Riot changed and explained the plan. "Word on the street is those booming sounds in the jungle are the Karnayers unloading their apex soldiers called Abominations. We're to go in, not engage, and collect as much intel as we can."

"Abominations, huh?" Wang said, shaking his head. "Why can't we ever go up against an enemy called the 'puppy people' or 'butterfly beauties'?"

"That's what I said." Riot grinned as she pulled her boots on.

A patrol of Trilords walked by, nodding to the men, then trying to get a look past them at a changing Riot.

"Nothing to see here. Move along, move along." Vet scowled at the larger alien species with his one good eye. "Keep going."

"Hey, my eyes are up here, perverts." Wang extended his arms to try to make a larger shield to block Riot. "You've never seen a woman change before?"

Rizzo ushered the amused Trilord patrol along with a wave of his hands.

"Some people," Vet huffed.

Riot smiled to herself as she grabbed her warhammer and placed it in the holder on her back. The handle of the weapon stuck up over her right shoulder. The armor that had been torn and punctured a few hours before had now been repaired.

Evonne handed Riot her helmet, as well as a Villain Pulse Rifle. "I brought your normal gear; however, now that I understand the mission is to be a recon trek, perhaps I should have brought a rifle with a more powerful scope, such as the Longshot 1000 Corporal Vetash seems to prefer."

"This will be fine," Riot said, accepting the weapon. "Our helmets will be able to zoom in for us, and Vet has the sniper rifle. We can use his scope if we need to."

"Understood," Evonne said, stepping back from Riot now that she was fully clothed.

"All right, Wolves," Riot said, placing herself in front

of her crew. "I know it's not really our style, but we're going to do this quietly. Into the jungle, gain intel, and then we're out. Oohrah?"

"Oohrah!" Vet and Wang said at once.

Rizzo pounded his right fist against his chest.

From around the corner of the building, Ketrick appeared, with Rippa right behind him. The larger Trilord held his signature staff blaster weapon in his right hand, face smeared with blood-red paint.

Rippa wore light combat armor with a heavy blaster in her hands. The weapon looked like a rocket launcher on crack cocaine.

"In and out, no fighting, we were never there," Riot repeated for Ketrick and Rippa's sake.

"My middle name is stealth," Ketrick said while he twitched his eyebrows up and down.

Rippa rolled her eyes as the group headed down the hill for the city gates. All around them, human, Trilord, and Grovothe were working side by side to prepare the city for an attack.

Grovothe mech pilots ran to their twenty-foot suits of armor, making last minute checks. Trilords stored water around the city in strategic places to put out fires.

Marines manned the walls and fixed stationary weapons on the battlements and on the tops of buildings and structures to repel the attack.

Nods and waves were exchanged from nearly everyone who saw them pass, regardless of their alien species. Word had spread through the ranks of both aliens and Marines about the insane Riot and her War Wolves.

"This is how it should be, right?" Wang said out loud. "I mean, everyone working together, regardless of background, race, or religion."

"It should be this way," Ketrick agreed. "But it seems only in the very worst of times will beings be willing to put aside their differences. It takes a catastrophic event such as this before we can see through the veil of hate and judgment."

"If we could always work like this, imagine what we could accomplish," Vet said.

Riot took a moment to reflect on their words and agree. They were right. It seemed not only Earth, but also the universe was a distrusting and judgmental place. How far could they come if they put that aside and judged people on their actions instead of on the preconceived notions of what they must be.

"All right, guys. You're all getting too deep for me," Riot said, placing her helmet on her head. "Eyes open. Here we go."

20

The dense jungle interior was made worse with the time of day as evening advanced. Riot led her unit with Wang. Ketrick, Rippa, Doctor Miller, and Evonne walking in the middle, while Rizzo and Vet brought up the rear.

Strange sounds in the jungle soon took precedence over the sounds of the booming coming from the Karnayer troops. A dozen smoke curls still lifted into the sky, but the constant noise that had heralded their arrival had finally silenced.

Alien chirps and howls drifted to Riot's ears from the jungle night life. Some animals had gone to sleep, while other nocturnal creatures were only beginning their day.

Aided by the night vision option in their heads-up display, Riot was able to see into the darkness like it was as bright as day.

"Do you think we can rename them?" Wang asked as he traveled by Riot's side along a rarely used trail Ketrick knew. "Why do we have to call them Abominations? Let's ratchet down the creep factor and just call them Smoochies or PLDs."

"What does PLD stand for?" Riot asked.

"Poor Life Decisions," Wang explained. "I mean, come on, we can call them whatever we want, right?"

"I guess," Riot said with a shrug, her mind less on the conversation and more on the jungle around her. "Whatever floats your boat."

"Maybe I should wait to see them before coming up with a cute name," Wang said, speaking more to himself than anyone else. "Or I could just call them bit—"

"Projected distance to the smokestacks is just under a mile," Evonne said via the units' comms. "We should be able to get a visual on them soon."

"Right," Riot answered before she began doling out orders. "Vet, take Rippa, Ketrick, and Rizzo along the right. Find a spot to hole up and gather as much intel as you can. Remember, do not engage. We are here, observing only."

"Roger that," Vet said over the comms as he and those with him peeled off to the right.

Ketrick caught Riot's eye and gave her a wink before he followed Vet.

"Let's get off the trail and head into the bush." Riot looked over to Evonne and Doctor Miller, who followed behind. "Wang, you bring up the rear; Evonne and Cupcake in the middle."

Wang immediately turned to take up the rear position as Riot led the group deeper into the jungle. The brush was so thick at times, Riot had to turn sideways. Vines hung down from trees whose roots travelled over the ground like a swarm of snakes.

Leaves ranging from the size of raindrops to cymbals made seeing harder than Riot imagined. At this point, they would be able to hear the enemy before they saw them.

Riot was right. Within a few more minutes of travel, a dull hum met their ears. It sounded as out of place in the jungle as an elephant at a high school. Only then did Riot realize the sounds of animal life in the jungle had completely died; only the hum remained, and with it, a sense of despair.

It sounded like an overpowered electrical grid teaming with energy. Riot lifted her hand to the others following behind her, then gave the sign for them to stay while she went on.

"I don't understand those hand signals," Doctor Miller whispered over the comms. "What do you want us to do?"

"I want you to be quiet and stay here," Riot growled.

"Oh, right." Doctor Miller and the others squatted down on the jungle ground. "Sorry."

Riot focused her attention on moving forward. With her Villain Pulse Rifle out in front of her, she carefully crossed the terrain. She made sure to keep her feet off any branches or leaves that would sound a crunch. She came around a massive tree as wide as Ketrick and as tall as Vikta. On the other side, she got her first look at the Abomination horde.

Riot's stomach clenched. She hunched down, making herself as small a target as possible. A newly made clearing had opened up in front of her. Jungle trees littered the ground, while others had been carted away, creating a staging ground for the Karnayer army.

Large transport ships lay in a line at the rear of the gathering, with an army of creatures lined up in front of them. These aliens had to be the Abominations Admiral Tricon was talking about.

They were stationed in a dozen square uniformed ranks right in front of the transport ships. The smoke that still rose into the air was due to what looked like chimneys in the center of each transport ship. The smoke rose high into the sky, as noises like hammering came from deep within the bellies of the ships.

Normal Karnayer soldiers dressed all in black patrolled the perimeter here and there, but the real threat was the Abomination soldiers. They were what looked like corpses from dozens of alien species. Some were short and thick like the Grovothe, others were tall like the Trilords. Some were huge beasts built like bears, while other were short with six arms.

Despite their different organic appearances, they had all been equipped with metal appendages. Some had metal parts covering their heads and torsos, and others had steel arms and legs, while still others seemed as though they were almost entirely machines save for a single eye, an arm, a leg, or a shoulder.

The inhuman hum came from the standing Abomination army. Not a single one of the soldiers moved, but the sound still emanated from the centers of their bodies like some kind of inhuman choir lending their voices to a macabre hymn.

Each one of the Abominations shared the exact same green glow that came from their eyes. Whether their eye was machine-made or organic, a dull, green glow Riot had become familiar with emanated from their eyes.

Magic is controlling them somehow, Riot said to herself. *These Karnayer sons of biscuits have figured out how to meld machines with the dead and bring them together using magic.*

"Are you seeing this?" Vet's voice came over the comms. His tone was one part wonder, one part determination.

"I'm seeing it." Riot's eyes roved over the gathered horde. "There has to be thousands of them."

"Thousands of zombie terminators," Vet breathed. "Check out their skin. The organic parts that are left are decomposing and rotting into their machine hides."

Riot zoomed in. Vet was right. Whatever organic pieces of the Abominations that remained were rotting and withered.

"I'm counting twelve groups of about a thousand each," Riot said over the comms. "What's your count?"

"Same," Vet answered. "Don't forget the Karnayer soldiers or the hammering coming from the insides of the transport ships. They're making something in there, and it can't be good."

Riot's eyes drifted back to the open transport doors, where the smoke and harsh rings of iron workers hard at their craft sounded out.

"Riot," Vet's voice came through, stressed, "I think—"

Boom! Boom! Boom!

The previously quiet night erupted with shots coming from Riot's right where Vet and his unit peered through the foliage. Bright green and red bolts flashed through the night.

The Abomination soldiers closest to the conflict hummed to life. As if they shared a single thought, they charged into the jungle's interior toward Vet and the rest of the unit. Rippa's blue weaponsfire and Ketrick's yellow blaster rang out with their booms and thumping sounds, respectively.

"Vet! Ketrick!" Riot yelled over the comms. Her yells would have been dampened by the weapons discharging two hundred yards to her right. "Anyone— do you copy?"

"Riot." Ketrick's voice yelled over the comms as he struggled for breath. "Run!"

No freaking way, Riot thought. *No chance in hell am I leaving them behind.*

Riot pushed her way back through the dense jungle foliage, heart beating in a quick deep tempo. She reached Wang and the others a moment later. Her heads-up display painted the waiting trio in a light as bright as day.

"You heard everything over the comms," Riot told the three nodding heads. "Bubbles, head back to the city and tell them a force of Karnayer and Abomination soldiers twelve thousand strong are on the way. Wang, Evonne, with me."

Riot didn't wait to see what their reaction would be; there was no time. Instead of waiting to hear a response, she crashed back into the jungle depths, headed for the location where she had last seen Vet and the others.

The fighting had intensified to the extent that there were no further pauses in weaponsfire, just a steady stream of loud explosions echoing through the jungle.

"Rippa, Rizzo, Vet, Ketrick," Riot said through panting breaths. "Do you copy?"

No response.

A moment later, the exchange of weaponsfire died.

The turn of events made Riot add speed to her strides. She ripped through vines that tore at her armor and over bushes seeking to impede her progress. She could hear Evonne and Wang crashing through the foliage behind her.

A second later, Riot burst into a clearing still smoking from the fire fight that had taken place a moment before. She was just in time to see Vet and Rizzo caught in a stranglehold by a massive Abomination with meaty hands and a domed head. Rippa lay unconscious, being dragged back to the Abomination lines by a pair of Karnayer soldiers, while Ketrick was on the ground, struggling to regain his feet under the onslaught of a dozen Abominations of varying sizes and races.

21

"Evonne, get Vet and Rizzo." Riot leveled her Villain Pulse Rifle and opened fire on the Abominations surrounding Ketrick. "Wang, get Rippa out of here."

Her aim was perfect. She hit an Abomination between its green eyes with a burst of fire and took another one in the chest with a shot that should have been enough to kill anything.

Instead of her targets falling over dead, they redirected their attention from a bloody Ketrick at their feet and moved to intercept Riot.

"Run!" Ketrick screamed, spitting blood from broken lips. "Riot, run!"

He was only wasting his breath, and somehow, Riot thought he knew that. She wasn't going to leave him or any of the soldiers under her command. If they were going down, then they were all going down together.

The Abominations ran at her, corpses that were part decaying alien and part machine. Riot pressed her finger on the trigger, going full auto. Red weaponsfire splashed across her targets. Her weapon opened up charred holes when she hit a portion of the Abominations' flesh and was absorbed when it hit their armor. Still, they came.

No screams or cries of war left the lips of the Abominations. Only the same dull hum of constant energy. Riot wasn't sure if that was actually scarier than hearing the grunts or roars from her enemies.

Out of the corner of her eye, she saw Evonne and Wang having more luck than she was at the moment. Evonne had managed to free Vet and Rizzo, who fell gasping to the ground. The AI was using pure strength as opposed to a weapon to overcome the Abomination.

Wang was up against a pair of dark-armored Karnayer soldiers that could actually be killed. Two well-placed bursts from his weapon and they were corpses smoking on the jungle floor.

Riot said a silent prayer, grateful that at least her counterparts had succeeded. The Abominations running at her moved out of the way for those among their order who carried blasters. The weapons had been fitted into the machine parts of their bodies on their arms or up from their shoulders. These weapons seemed to be nothing but random fittings of blasters or blades.

BOOM! BOOM! BOOM! BOOM!

Riot sent a salvo of red rounds into any and every section of the charging figures she thought may be susceptible to fire. She hit one in the neck, another in the kneecap, and a third in the eye.

Her attempt seemed to only piss off the Abominations as they continued toward her. Those enemies with blaster-equipped weapons fired at Riot. Green rounds struck her in the abdomen and her left leg.

"Rrrrrrr…" Riot grunted as she went down to one knee. The entire time her gaze never left the targets rushing toward her. Despite her best efforts, the most she managed was to make one stumble as a round collided with its left ankle. "Die, you sons of biscuits!"

They were about to reach her. Knives, blades, and claws extended toward her, along with a dozen different alien appendages that reached for her face.

Here we go again. Riot dropped her Villain Pulse Rifle and reached for her warhammer that sat in its place across her back. *Why can't anything be easy?*

The steady hum coming from their bodies was the only thing heralding the charge of the Abominations.

"Come on!" Riot screamed, doing her best to get herself psyched for the fight. "Get some!"

Mere feet from colliding with the Abominations, a stream of searing hot fire erupted in front of Riot. A wall of flames burst to life, separating Riot from the dozen Abominations in front of her. A handful of the half-corpse, half-machines were even caught in the flames, their organic parts melting off their steel frame.

Riot looked up as a whoosh of wings reached her ears. Vikta's massive figure was on an upward swing before the dragon turned back for another pass.

"I had them!" Riot yelled at the dragon. There was nothing but joy in her voice despite her words. "I had them just where I wanted them."

Ketrick was limping his way around the wall of fire on Riot's left. Wang and Evonne were doing the same thing on the right. Rippa was the only one who seemed to be fine. Evonne was carrying Rizzo, and Wang had an arm wrapped around a limping Vet.

More and more Abominations, as well as Karnayer soldiers, were running toward their position. Vikta let out a roar, sending another line of flames alongside the already burning fire wall.

For the moment, the only thing the Abominations and Karnayers were concerned about was the colossal dragon shooting flames at them. Enemy weaponsfire was solely concentrated on the dragon for a moment.

"We should go," Ketrick said, spitting out a mouthful of blood. "Vikta's buying us the time we need to get back to the city."

"Good, let's—"

"Riot!" a scream from someone on the other side of the flames interrupted Riot's next words. "Riot, you coward! I know that's you!"

Riot didn't have to wonder who was calling her by

name from the Karnayer forces. She recognized Alveric's voice. Her eyes searched through the flickering fire wall separating the two factions. She finally found the tall, blue-skinned Karnayer on the opposite side of the flames.

"What? Who is it? Alveric, is that you?" Riot shouted. She cupped her right hand to the side of her helmet. "It's hard to hear you above the sound of all of your Abominations humming. You're really going to have to speak up. How's the wound on your face healing, by the way?"

"Run! Run back to your city and supposed safety," Alveric screamed in anger, ignoring her question. "We will kill you there within the hour. Run! Run, human! You and your allies will burn together before the sun rises!"

Vikta did another pass, barrel rolling through the enemy fire that was peppering her. The flame wall came to life again. As much as Riot wanted to stay and trade words with Alveric, every moment she forced Vikta to remain and defend them was another chance that a Karnayer round could wound the dragon. Riot wasn't willing to bet on Vikta's safety. Not like that.

"I'll look for you on the battlefield," Riot yelled back to Alveric. "I'll be the one holding a warhammer with a pile of dead Karnayers at my feet."

Riot turned back to her team. The nanites were already hard at work in everyone's bodies. Even Rizzo was already moving in Evonne's arms. Evonne still held the wounded pilot like a groom ready to walk over the threshold with his wife.

"Let's go," Riot ordered her unit. "Double time, back to the city. They won't be far behind."

Riot fell in line with her squad as they ran back through the jungle to the city. Riot hated having to try to carry on a conversation while running, but she had to be sure Doctor Miller had gotten the message through to the city.

"Evonne, patch me through to General Armon," Riot panted as she concentrated on where she was placing her feet.

"Done," Evonne responded back in her calm, non-exerted voice despite the fact she was outpacing them all.

"General," Riot gasped as she urged her team on. "We have an enemy force, maybe thirteen thousand strong, made up of soldiers that'll need heavy weaponsfire and incendiary rounds to be taken out."

"Roger that," General Armon's voice came back over the comms, clear and calm. "Doctor Miller gave us a report. We'll be ready. Just get you and your team back safe."

"Roger." Riot forced herself to breathe past her burning lungs.

Vikta flew above them in circles, dipping back every so often to light another flame wall and protect their retreat.

I'm going to have to get Vikta a treat or something to say thank you. Riot's mind started to wander as she pushed her body to the limit. *Do they even make dragon treats? If they did, would they be the same shape as a dog treat, only bigger?*

"There it is," Vet huffed over his comms.

Through the thick foliage, Riot could see glimpses of the city walls. She wondered how long they had been running while she'd allowed her mind to wander. Riot was at the rear of the group, constantly looking behind her into the jungle depths. She was lucky that, thus far, she had not seen any signs of pursuing enemies. She had a sneaking suspicion she had Vikta to thank for that.

Riot and her team came to a skidding stop in front of the Trilord walls. Riot removed her helmet as the gates to the city swung open. The warm night air hit her face. Whereas helmet's heads-up display painted the darkness as bright as day made her eyes blink to give her pupils time to adjust.

The night on Hoydren was still warm, but a cool breeze touched her sweaty face and sent her short hair into a frenzy. Riot followed her unit into the city grounds, already barking orders to her team.

"Is everyone okay?" Riot looked from one face to the next. A series of nods returned her question. Not only were these the toughest men and women she had ever served with, but the addition of the nanites also made them that much harder to seriously injure.

"We're good to go," Wang said from his spot next to Rizzo. "Where do you want us?"

Riot was about to start going over the plan, when Colonel Harlan appeared with a force of heavily armored Marines behind him. "Glad to see you all back in one piece. General Armon and Admiral Tricon are taking the fight to the sky. I'll be coordinating our defense on the ground. I'd like Killa and her Trilords to defend the south wall facing the jungle, and you, Riot, to defend the east gate."

They both knew what he was asking without having to voice their thoughts. The south wall would be the first area to receive enemy contact, sure, but the real fight would be for the main entrance to the city— the east gate.

"Done." Riot looked to the colonel through the darkness. Torches set into the walls near the gates sent shadows playing across his face. "We'll hold the gates."

"I know you will," Colonel Harlan said with a nod. "Admiral Tricon is leaving us his mechs for the defense. They'll be air-dropping in soon. You'll also have a division of Grovothe shock troops at your command. I have Killa's Trilords placed across the wall with her and the Marines, but if you need additional help, let me know, and I'll re-route a reinforcement class to your position. We'll use Ketrick and his dragons as a roving support band where the fighting is the worst."

"Understood," Riot said, thinking back to how

difficult it had been to take down a single Abomination soldier. "Colonel Harlan."

"Yes, Riot?" the colonel asked.

"Tell everyone we'll need to only use the weapons capable of making the biggest booms in this fight. Small arms fire and blaster rounds just glance off these new soldiers."

Colonel caught the intensity in Riot's eye. "We'll roll out the big guns. What were you thinking: mines, grenades, mortars, rockets?"

"All of them," Riot said, and nodded along with each item on the colonel's list. "We'll need them all."

22

I t was Riot's show now. She was in charge of her crew, along with the squad of mechs and the Grovothe division of shock troops. Luckily for her, the commander in charge of the Grovothe shock troops assigned to the wall was an old friend. Brimley, the pilot that had once been in Rippa's mech unit during the fight against the Zenoth, was now geared up to fight on foot.

"No armored unit to lead into battle this time around?" Riot asked Brimley as the two shook hands. "I thought you'd be in a mech the next time I saw you."

"Oh, I'm still planning to fight the battle from the inside of a mech, but I'm going to position the shock troops first and act as a stationary Fortress class mech inside the wall," Brimley said, releasing Riot's hand. "You look confused."

"I am," Riot admitted. "What's a Fortress class mech?"

"You'll see," Brimley said with a wink. "They should be dropping the mech suits any time now. Until then, let me know where you want the shock troops, and I'll place them as needed."

"Right," Riot said, and as she was about to dole out orders, Wang and Rizzo came up to her, carrying boxes of anti-personal mines. She shifted to direct them before answering Brimley's question.

Rizzo pretended to trip, and he careened into Wang. Rizzo pushed the Marine who was carrying his own crate of anti-personal mines as if with a single sneeze they would go off.

"Stop it! What are you doing?" Wang said as his face transitioned from a look of concentration to utter terror. "Not funny. Not funny at all, man. We could detonate these things with one wrong move."

Rizzo rolled his eyes. The two Marines continued their approach to Riot. Wang's hands slightly trembling, while Rizzo carried the crate like a pizza box.

"Good," Riot said to her Marines. "Get Evonne, Vet, and Doctor Miller to help you place them. Hurry, we don't know how much time we have left. And put them far enough away from the wall so none of the mechs will accidentally step on one."

Wang and Rizzo hurried through the open gates to obey.

"Sorry about that," Riot said as she turned back to address Brimley's question. "We'll need the Grovothe shock troops on the wall over the gate with whatever weapons they have that pack the biggest punch. I'll be up there with them, with the rest of my team."

"Understood," Brimley said, and with a tight salute, she ran toward the rest of the shock troops, explaining their positions and the orders Riot had given.

"Vikta says the main Karnayer force is twenty minutes from arriving at the south wall." Ketrick approached Riot as she made for the top of the wall. "I should stay here with you. I should be defending the wall with you."

"We both know your ability is needed to communicate with the dragons and lead them into the battle." Riot had said the words like she was convincing herself he couldn't be with her. "You just do your dragon thing and keep these Abominations off the wall."

"I'll be close, if you need me, Sorceress," Ketrick said, giving her one of his signature winks before leaving Riot to her next task.

Riot forced her feet to carry her upward until she came to the top of the wall, where the Grovothe shock troops were already preparing their defensive stations. Tripods were being erected to house massive armaments that looked like Gattling guns. Rocket launchers and stores of ammunition were being set up, along with crates of grenades.

This was going to be a very different fight from the previous one. The initial fight had been an aviation conflict, with the Karnayers swooping down on a near-defenseless city. Now, with Admiral Tricon and General Armon in the air, with Ketrick's dragons as a backup plan, they would be more than a match for the Karnayer destroyers.

This fight would depend solely on if they would be able to stop the Abomination army or not. A thought that disturbed Riot to no end was the fact that the Abomination soldiers wouldn't go down. Even with Vikta's intense flames, had they actually caught on fire? The organic matter on their bodies melted from the heat, but did the metal portion of their bodies go down at all?

Riot couldn't remember.

"Riot, I'm checking in over the comps to make sure we are linked and can speak to one another over the distance of the city," Killa's said in Riot's ear. "These comps are truly amazing."

"Comms, Killa, comms," Riot said over the comm. "Yes, I can hear you, loud and clear."

"Amazing," Killa said again. "Commander Killa of the Trilord Savage army, over and out."

"Killa, you really gotta keep chatter on the comms to a minimum," Riot said, shaking her head as she looked out over the wall into the darkness. "I get that you're excited, but you can just say 'over' or not say anything, and that would be fine, as well."

"Oh, right. Over," Killa said again.

"Is Queen Revna in the capitol building?" Riot asked, braving another verbal download from Killa. "I haven't seen her."

"She is, for the time being. However, it's not in her nature to stay safe while others risk their lives for the city," Killa answered. "She'll be out soon."

Riot nodded along with Killa's words. More respect for Ketrick's mother grew deep inside of her. She had no doubt the queen would be out giving encouragement and even helping where she could when the fighting started. She was that kind of leader.

Riot took another second to look over the section of the wall she was in charge of guarding. The jungle opened up to her right. Directly in front of her, a wide dirt path led from the city as far as the eye could see. Below her, thick double doors made of wood and laced with iron gave entrance into the city. Whether the wall had been raised or not, she couldn't remember, but at her section of the city, it rose three stories into the air. At that moment, it didn't seem high enough.

Aircrafts coming in sounded in the night sky.

Riot braced herself.

"Archangel transports approaching with the mechs and supplies," Rippa said over the comms. "Look at those beauties."

Riot squinted through the dark to see a long, thick ship come in. It was an exact replica of the one that had given them transport to the Zenoth home planet of

Raydon when they had made their attack on the Zenoth hives.

A door opened from the bottom of the Archangel transport. The craft lowered closer to the ground, now only a few stories over the wall. Three bulky forms dropped from the ship, one touching down just inside the gate, while two others dropped to the ground outside of the wall.

BAM! BAM! BAM!

A cheer went up from the Grovothe as they witnessed their war machines enter the battlefield. All along the south wall, similar instances were taking place as pilots manning Archangel transports dropped mechs onto the ground.

"Heard you could use some support," Atlas's gruff, no-nonsense voice sounded over the comms.

Atlas was the third member in Rippa's original party. The fourth, Ragnar, had died on the assault on the Zenoth.

"Good to hear from you, Atlas," Rippa said with genuine joy in her voice. "Let's gear up."

Riot watched as Grovothe pilots jumped out of Rippa's and Brimley's mech suits to allow the pilots their cockpits. Rippa's and Atlas's mechs outside of the wall were similar to the ones Riot had been accustomed to seeing—twenty-foot armored tanks with arms and legs that looked like giant robots ready for war.

Each of their suits was equipped with a rail gun on

top of their forearms. A laser beam could be shot from the helmet. A flamethrower and claws could be extended from their hands.

These intimidating figures were known as Juggernaut class mechs. In their own right, they were brutal machines used to deal death and destruction out on the battlefield. The mech that dropped just inside the wall of the Trilord city was something else entirely.

The Fortress class mech was anchored in a wide base with what looked like tank treads on the bottom. It was as tall as the Juggernaut class mechs, but the upper body portion was heavy. No arms extended from the machine, just two massive square rocket housings, and below that, two Gatling-type guns.

It was clear to Riot that the Fortress class mech was made for one thing: destruction. Brimley climbed in, strapping herself in the center of the machine where a cockpit closed to protect her. She maneuvered the machine slowly to an overwatch position just above the wall.

"Atlas and I will keep anything from reaching the gates," Rippa said into the comms as if asking Riot for permission. "Brimley can assume an overwatch position in the Fortress mech, if that's okay with you, Riot?"

"Sounds good." Riot looked over the wall to where her Marines were placing the mines a hundred yards from the city walls. "Rippa, Atlas, mark the spots on your heads-up displays where the mines are being laid. The last thing we need is you two going too far out and blowing a mine."

"Copy that," the two Grovothe pilots said in unison.

"Hey, what do you have there?" Riot looked over to a Grovothe shock trooper who was opening up a case of weapons that looked like a grenade launcher with three barrels at the end.

"It's a Buster300." The Grovothe looked at Riot with admiration in his heart. "Want to try one?"

"Buster300?" Riot said, accepting the weapon. "Hell yeah, I want to try it. You had me at 'Bust.' It'll make a good primary weapon to the warhammer on my back."

"Oh, you bet." The young Grovothe seemed eager to talk. He started rattling off the weapon's specs, something about clip size and firepower. Riot's attention drifted to a noise she caught on the breeze.

She tilted her head, trying to get a better angle to catch the sound.

"The Buster300 just came out of—"

Riot pressed her right extended pointer finger into the Grovothe's lips to quiet him. The Grovothe shock trooper took the hint and silenced with Riot's finger still on his mouth. His eyes were wide as he, too, picked up on the noise.

A dull hum wafted from the jungle, the smell of rotting corpses on the breeze.

23

"It's go-time," Riot said to the Grovothe in front of her, finally taking her finger off the shock trooper's lips. "Send the word down the line. No one fires until I tell them we're ready."

The Grovothe nodded violently before taking off at a run.

The chill that ran down Riot's spine was one of anxious anticipation. She placed her black-and-red helmet on her head. Her heads-up display once again made her view as clear as day.

"Everybody back inside the gates now," Riot said over the comms. "We're about to have company."

"Roger that," Vet responded through his own helmet.

"Riot, this is Killa," Killa said over her own comm. "We're getting a sound of something like humming from the south side. They're here."

"They'll hit you first, and then swing around to us," Riot said, watching her Marines, Doctor Miller, and Evonne sprint back to the gate. "Level them with your heavy weapons and let's hope between that and the mechs we have enough firepower to take them down."

Riot looked to the right and to the left of the wall. From either side, a dozen Grovothe shock troops looked at her for direction. Riot could hear her own unit closing the city gates below her and locking them in place.

Riot wasn't the best at giving motivational speeches, but right now, before all hell broke loose, she realized these soldiers needed a pep talk. Word had spread of what they were about to face. The Abominations were something none of these soldiers wanted to go up against. Regardless, they were here, ready to die if need be.

The hum was now loud enough that every set of ears was picking up on the noise. Left unchecked, the warriors who had not yet encountered the Abomination horde were powerless to stop their imaginations from wandering, and fear grow within their hearts.

Riot realized she had to say something. If not for her, then for them. Fear was a cancer that, if left unchecked, would bring the greatest warrior to their knees.

"Listen up!" Riot shouted as she began walking up and down the wall. "I don't care if you're human,

Grovothe, Trilord, or some weird alien mix of all three. Today, we're in this together. We're in this because there are planets left in the universe who refuse to die alone. There are those of us who see the value of lifting each other up and standing as one. Today, that's us. In one voice, we tell the Karnayers that they've picked the wrong planets to mess with. Today, we are telling the Karnayers it is not our end, but theirs. Today, we rise up and make them rethink ever showing their faces in our part of the universe again!"

A cheer erupted from those inside the city, a cheer too loud to have just been her own section on the wall. Too late Riot realized Killa had broadcasted her message to every soldier in the city.

"Oohrah!" the Marines shouted.

"Kill, kill, kill!" the Trilords roared.

"Aaroo!" the Grovothes added.

"If we die today, then we die together!" Rippa screamed over her comms, caught up in the intensity of Riot's speech.

"Why does she always have to go so dark?" Wang whispered over the comms. "Why can't we just all *live* together?"

"They're here," Killa said at the same time as weaponsfire lit up the night sky.

From her vantage point, Riot could look behind her to the right and see a flurry of weaponsfire cascading down over the wall and into the jungle interior below.

The mech unit stationed outside the wall lent their firepower to the cause.

The sound was so intense, Riot was sure she would have gone deaf, had it not been for the protection her helmet provided.

Dat-dat-dat-dat-dat

The new Grovothe weapons added their own unique sounds to the noise of war, and the cacophony a large engagement brought with it tore across the night sky. Riot had been in enough battles by now to know what to expect. The sounds dampened by her helmet were like hearing thunder and lightning exploding overhead, as if Zeus himself was hurling his lightning bolts just feet away from her position.

Bright colors from the weaponsfire raced across the sky. Red fire from the Marines and the repurposed weapons from the Syndicate mixed with the yellow blaster fire of the Trilords and the blue laser rounds from the Grovothe mechs.

The Abominations and the Karnayer soldiers answered back with their own green rounds shooting upward and aiming at the defenders on the wall.

Everything in Riot told her she needed to run over and join the fight. Her muscles tightened, only relaxing when she concentrated all of her willpower on the action. The muscles in her shoulders bunched up like rocks.

Riot could feel the tension and energy in the air as her Marines and the Grovothe force around her looked back to the right and the south wall. They all wanted to go help.

"We're going to have our opportunity in a few minutes," Riot said, embracing the part of her she needed to be in that moment, the part that welcomed a fight. "Lock and load. When they get here, we hold the gates at all costs."

"Oorah!"

"Aaroo!"

"There's thousands of them," Killa shouted over the comms. Her voice was far from fear; it was loud and excited. "Weaponsfire aren't having any effect on the Abominations. The mechs using the blue laser beams from their helmets seem like the only thing able to keep them back."

"Do you need additional support?" Colonel Harlan said over the comms. "Give me the word, and I can route a squad of Trilords over to your position."

"We're holding now," Killa said before static covered her voice over the comms. She came back a moment later, loud and clear. "The Abominations aren't going down, but neither can they climb the walls. Riot, they're swinging around to the east gate!"

"Let them come!" Riot roared over the comms. Her heart raced as she scanned the outside of the wall through her heads-up display. "We're ready for them."

"There!" Vet shouted over the comms in his helmet. "To the right, just in the jungle."

Riot allowed her heads-up display to see what her

eyes could not. Dozens of outlined enemies showed on her screen as they emerged from the jungle's depths.

Heat signatures weren't present amongst the cold steel corpses the Abominations were made of, but her heads-up display was able to track movement. They emerged from the jungle depths like a wave of blood oozing from an open wound.

They walked at first, and then ran.

"Open up, boys and girls!" Riot aimed her new Grovothe weapons over the wall. The bulky Buster300 felt good in her hands. "Let's give them a warm, bloody welcome."

BOOM! BOOM! BOOM!

Riot aimed at a particularly small Abomination soldier who looked like a grub equipped with mechanical arms and legs. She caught the monster in the face, as well as center body mass. Her target stumbled at first, but just kept moving forward.

All around her, Grovothe and Marines were reveling in the target-rich environment. Despite the level of sheer firepower being directed at the Abomination horde, the results were minimal at best. A few enemy soldiers were having a hard time moving forward under the hose of weaponsfire but none of their number remained down for the count.

The two mechs in front of the gate piloted by Rippa and Atlas stood with their arms pointing forward. Gauss rounds pumped from the twin cannons on the tops of their forearms.

"Concentrate all your firepower on those closest to the wall, on the right," Riot screamed into her comm to be heard over the weaponsfire. "Make them swing wider left and into the road where our mines are set up!"

Immediately, everyone obeyed. Blue and red rounds slammed into the Abominations closest to the wall on the right corner. Brimley focused her Fortress mech's fire on those Abominations as well, and let loose with her twin Gatling-type guns.

Dat-dat-dat-dat-dat-dat!

The sound was music to Riot's ears as the Fortress class mech opened fire behind her. Brimley's aim took her rounds high over the heads of Riot and the rest of the team and up over the wall.

Abominations fell, got back up and fell again, only to be pinned on the ground by more weaponsfire. But Riot recognized a fatal flaw in their plan. For the time being, they were managing to hold at bay a few hundred Abominations, but what about when the rest of the Karnayers' resurrected force spilled from around the southern corner?

"Ketrick, can you do a few passes along the southern wall?" Killa shouted into her comms. "The Abominations have reached the wall. They can't climb over, but the mechs in front of us are in danger of being overrun."

"On our way," Ketrick responded.

Riot's right shoulder shook as she pumped round

after round of blue blaster fire from her Grovothe-made Buster300 into the oncoming Abomination horde. High above her in the night sky, Ketrick led a wing of dragons swooping down alongside the southern wall and painting the jungle forests in flames.

A cheer erupted from the Trilords and Marines on that side of the wall.

Riot felt a swell of hope as she hammered another dozen rounds into a large Abomination that had at one time been something close to humanoid. She focused her fire on its right fleshy knee, obliterating the appendage. The half-machine, half-corpse fell to the ground, only to begin crawling forward over the hard-packed dirt. Metal fingers clawed into the earth as it continued its journey forward.

Riot's weapon soon made a loud clicking sound, signaling it was dry. All around her, Grovothes were exchanging thick mags at the base of their weapon for mags that were full; they threw the empty magazines on the floor atop the wall and reached into crates for new ones.

Some of the Grovothe shock troops carried the same weapon she did. The trio of thick blasters on the end of their weapon rotated, taking turns to hurl blue bolts at the enemy. Other Grovothe-manned massive cannons sat on tripods, and still others, what looked like RPGs, rested on their shoulders.

"Riot, we're about to have a problem," Rippa said from the safety of her mech on the outside of the wall.

"Of course we are," Riot said, looking to Rippa's mech and following its line of sight into the jungle to pick up whatever it was she had caught sight of. "We're being attacked by the living dead on an alien planet where fast food doesn't exist. I would call that a huge problem. I don't think it can get much worse."

"No, I mean, look." Rippa pointed into the jungle depths.

Thousands more of the Abominations created by the strange magic the Karnayers possessed had just emerged, and were now sprinting toward them from the jungle depths.

Thus far, the Abominations spilling over from the south wall had not been equipped with range weapons. A fact Riot should have picked up on, and in turn, expected there to be a reason why.

The force emerging from the jungle was not only ten times as large as the one coming from the south, but they were also all equipped with various blasters attached to their arms.

"Riot, I think it's worse. And what's 'fast food'?" Rippa asked as she pivoted to meet this new threat.

Riot ducked as a salvo of green enemy fire erupted from the new force.

"Ask me again when we get through this," Riot said over the comms as her mind struggled to compose a new plan.

BOOM!

The first anti-personnel mine in the dirt road leading to the main gate erupted in a shower of dust and broken metal body parts. Abominations were tossed into the air like rag dolls. In turn, they fell to the ground, only to detonate more of the mines.

BOOM! BOOM! BOOM! BOOM!

More and more of the explosions discharged, bringing a cheer to the throats of the defenders on the wall.

Riot, on the other hand, understood that the temporary victory would still not hold back the thousands of Abominations for long. She looked to her right where her crew had taken up positions on the wall. Vet, Wang, Rizzo, and even Evonne, were firing their own weapons into the crowd of gathered enemies, while Doctor Miller ran ammo supply packs to the Grovothe troops.

"We're not going to be able to hold them back once the mines are depleted," Evonne said in her matter-of-fact Australian accent. "I'm not trying to be pessimistic, only factual."

"Rippa, Atlas," Riot said as even more mines detonated. "You'll need to use your laser beams soon. Brimley, those rockets you're carrying, make them count."

"Roger," Rippa, Atlas, and Brimley all said at once.

"The beams our mechs are equipped with will run hot and powerful, but not for long," Rippa reminded Riot.

Riot thought back to the time she witnessed the powerful blue laser beams shoot from the eyes of the mech's helmet. While Riot had been on Raydon fighting the Zenoth with the Grovothe, she had come to respect the weapons.

"I understand," Riot said over the comms as she stood up to aim her weapon at the road once more. "Do what you can."

An eerie silence settled across the front of the gates. Those Abominations that had been spilling around the south corner had stopped. A thick cloud of smoke and dirt from the detonated land mines made visibility impossible for more than a few hundred yards in front of the gates.

Riot breathed steadily. The constant hum of the

Abominations was the only thing to tell her they were still out there.

In front of Riot stood Rippa's mech on the right and Atlas's on the left. Each of the hulking armor tanks practically vibrated with energy.

Riot thought about requesting a fly-by from Ketrick, Vikta, and his dragons, but she knew she needed to save the call. She also still had the option of asking for reinforcements from Colonel Harlan. Again, she decided to wait for a moment when there was no other option.

Inside her helmet, Riot could hear her pulse pounding in her head. Seconds ticked by slower and slower as all eyes on the wall tried penetrating the haze of smoke and dirt. A blue round fired from somewhere to her left. Riot looked over to see a fidgety Grovothe Shock trooper looking around sheepishly.

"We'll hold," Riot said to everyone. "Don't fire until you can see them. When they come, send everything we've got that goes 'boom.'"

"There!" Wang shouted over his comms. "Twelve o'clock and—limping toward us?"

A single Abomination came out of the haze. Wang was right. Instead of running, it was walking toward them with a hitch in its step. Then hundreds more Abominations materialized from the smoke, sprinting forward.

"Now!" Riot ordered as she opened fire into the throng. All around her, weapons were unloaded.

The Grovothe abandoned smaller firearms for mortars. The rounds sailed from stationary tubes up and over the wall, into the Abomination ranks.

Green fire from the enemy splattered against the wall, taking out an unsuspecting Grovothe standing next to Riot with a round to his head. The soldier fell backwards off the wall, never to rise again.

Rippa and Atlas opened up with the blue laser beams from their mech's helmets.

VRRRROOOOOOOOM!

Thus far, the laser beams were the most effective weapons Riot had seen used on the enemy. The cobalt blue streams of energy were able to cut through both the organic and metal sections of the Abomination soldiers.

Rippa focused her laser on a rather large creature with a massive torso and tiny metal legs. Her laser ate through the alien's midsection. She lowered her aim first, then raised it, cutting the Abomination completely in two.

Beside her, Atlas was having similar luck. Although their weapons were effective in taking an Abomination soldier out of the fight for good, the time in which they needed to focus and kill a single enemy was not going to win them the day. In the duration, the two Juggernaut class mechs had dispatched a handful of the Abominations. Running across the open road to the gates, the enemy was nearly on top of them.

"Brimley," Riot grunted as she lifted one of the

Grovothe's RPG-type weapons onto her right shoulder and took aim. "Now would be a good time to let those rockets loose."

"Roger that," Brimley said. "Locking onto multiple targets now, in three … two … one … kill time."

Rockets zipped down onto the wave of enemy Abominations. The enemy horde had nearly reached Rippa and Atlas, who stood right in front of the gates. Trails of smoke wafted from the afterburn of the small rockets as they all found a target.

BAM! BAM! BAM! BAM! BAM!

Each rocket struck its intended target, sending up a shower of dead matter and scrap metal. More cheers from the defenders on the wall rose up in an echo of shouts and yells.

The two dozen rockets that had found their marks had given everyone on the wall a sense of joy, except for Riot. She understood that ammunition was a dwindling commodity, especially among the Grovothe who did not have access to the unlimited power packs the Syndicate had introduced to Earth.

"How many more rounds like that do you have in your mech?" Riot asked Brimley over a private comm channel. "Tell me you can do that over and over again."

"Well, do you want me to lie to you, or do you want me to tell you I have one round like that left once I reload," Brimley replied. "I can have the second round reloaded in the next two minutes."

"Save them for when I give you the command. In

the meantime, let loose with those Gatling guns," Riot said, switching once again to the main channel. "Evonne, We're going to need your muscle at the gates soon. Get down there and brace the supports."

"Understood," Evonne's voice said over the blasts of weaponsfire.

Riot hefted the Grovothe rocket launcher onto her shoulder and aimed over the wall. She looked through a circular scope that popped out of the side of the thick barrel and focused on a shifty Abomination alien that had long metallic scythes for arms.

SHHHHHHHHHHOOOOOM!

Riot hit the button, sending the rocket forward. The recoil nearly took her off her feet. The rocket left a blue stream of smoke in its wake. Riot's aim was true as it collided with its target and sent the Abomination up in a cloud of dirt and smoke.

A decision needed to be made soon. The Abomination soldiers were going down under the onslaught of the heavy weapons Riot and her team defended the wall with, but they just weren't going down fast enough.

The hum the horde of robotic dead made as they crashed against Rippa and Atlas's mechs were maddening. The green blaster fire many of the Abomination soldiers used as fire against the Grovothe mechs simply splashed against their metal. The bladed hand weapons the Abominations brought to bear against the mechs, on the other hand, were more than capable of cutting through the steel.

"Off, you sick magically dead," Atlas grunted over the comms as he crushed one soldier under his boot and tried to shake off another from the opposite leg. "Fire and Claw, Major?"

"Fire and Claw," Rippa agreed over the comm as she opened a flame from the right hand of her mech. Three long blades sprouted from her other hand in between the knuckles of her closed fist. "Riot, they're past us now. We'll stay out here as long as we can, but the gates need to be braced."

"Roger that," Riot said, dropping her empty rocket launcher. She ducked under the edge of the fortification as another wave of green blaster fire peppered the wall around her. "Don't stay on the other side of the wall until your mech goes down. If you're going to be overwhelmed, you get to this side of the wall. That's an order, Major Rippa Gunna."

Riot felt like a parent scolding her young daughter when she used Rippa's full name. The fact was, Riot wondered if Rippa would ignore the order anyway and seek what she deemed a glorious death in battle.

These thoughts raced through Riot's mind as she hurried down the steps to the gates. The first wave of Abominations would reach them soon.

Riot took the steps down, two at a time. Right in the middle of the courtyard rising up like a statue of war,

Brimley slowly turned her Fortress class mech from side to side, sending a stream of fire into the horde.

Dat-dat-dat-dat-dat-dat!

Riot jumped the last few feet to the ground before sprinting over to the gate. Evonne stood bracing the city's entrance, one hand on each gate door, arms extended, legs staggered.

The Abominations hit the wooden gate so hard, Riot could see the wooden structure shudder. Evonne even took a step back from the violence of the impact. Riot slammed into the wooden door so hard, she thought she might have broken something. She shoved her left shoulder into the door, hoping to absorb some of the impact from the forces on the other side.

Even amongst the rockets and blaster fire going off in the background, Riot could hear the scraping of steel weapons on wood from the other side of the barrier.

This is it. Riot gritted her teeth as thoughts ran through her head a mile a minute. *This is where they break through and overrun the city. Time to call in the cavalry.*

25

At that moment, Evonne looked over to Riot from her position bracing the gates. The AI still hadn't been repaired from the previous fight. Her skin fell off her body and a portion of her face. The steel underneath grinned back at her like something from a nightmare.

"What are you doing?" Riot asked as her feet fought for traction in the dirt floor. "Why are you looking at me like that?"

"I understand you are feeling a tremendous amount of stress in this wartime environment," Evonne said as calm as if she were giving someone directions. "I thought a smile would be in order."

"No, stop it. You're just making things worse and freaking me out," Riot said, shaking her head. She opened up the comms channel in her helmet. "Colonel

Harlan we could use those reinforcements at the front gate, and Ketrick, it's time to bring the pain."

"Roger that, Riot," Colonel Harlan's steady voice said over the comms. "They're en route to you now."

"What do you mean by 'bring the pain'?" Ketrick's voice came over the comms, faint and distant as if a tremendous amount of wind was being rushed past.

"The dragons, Muscles." Riot couldn't tell if he was kidding with her or serious, but she suspected the former. "Get your Trilord Prince rear end over here and light up some of these suckers!"

"On our way!" Ketrick responded.

"Vet, Wang, Rizzo, Sunshine," Riot said into her comms as the wooden grates swayed and groaned with the pressure coming from the other side. "Get down here and help brace the gate."

A series of "Rogers" came over the comms.

That was it. Riot had played all her cards now. If they couldn't hold the position with the reinforcements coming, then the Trilord capital city would be overrun and the end would be near.

Thunk!

A curved steel blade penetrated the wooden gate, its tip suddenly appearing an inch away from Riot's face like some macabre magic trick. The gate creaked and bent again as if it were going to snap in half at any second.

Maybe you waited too long to ask for help, Riot thought. *Maybe this is how it was always supposed to be.*

Dying on the ground, alone. Well, not exactly alone. You have the smiling Terminator holding the gate by your side.

A rush of wings filled the night air as Ketrick's dragons flew overhead. Riot looked up in time to see the underbelly of a handful of different colored dragons soar by, led by Vikta and Ketrick. The sight was like some kind of weird rainbow as white, green, blue, yellow, red, purple, and orange serpentine bodies soared over the wall.

"I heard you need a hand, Little One," Ketrick said, laughing at his newly coined name for Rippa. "I must have killed two hundred of the Abominations by now. What's your meager count?"

"You're lucky you're on Vikta or I'd shoot you out of the sky and call it an accident," Rippa growled with a hint of merriment in her voice. "It's good to see you, you giant idiot."

"Clear the wall," Ketrick said to Rippa. "We'll begin our attack runs and try to buy you a brief rest."

Riot could hear the dragons begin their attack runs on the opposite side of the wall. At the same time, her crew arrived at the gates with the now-empty crates the Grovothe shock troops on the wall had used. Although they had once carried ammunition, they were sturdy enough to use as support.

"Good thinking." Riot moved out of the way to allow her Marines to stack the extra crates against the gates for an added barricade.

"I bet that's the first time anyone has said that to you, Vet," Wang said over his comms.

"Your mom said it last time she was in town," Vet said back without missing a beat.

"Really, you two?" Doctor Miller hefted her crate against the gate to the left of Evonne. "Even now?"

Always, Rizzo wrote over their heads-up display.

"Look!" Doctor Miller shouted.

Riot followed her gaze to the path that sloped up the hill toward the capitol building, where Queen Revna led a contingent of ten Trilord soldiers wearing the black dragon tattoos of her personal guard.

The queen wore battle gear of what looked like tough leather and iron. Strapped to her shoulder and forearms were a series of iron armor pieces. Over her ample chest she wore a black leather piece that came down to her wide hips and ended in a skirt.

The weapon she carried in her hands was unlike anything Riot had ever seen, and that was saying a lot, since Riot had seen machine corpses being brought back from the dead by green Karnayer magic.

In her right hand, Queen Revna carried a massive sword that was nearly as large as her body. The double-handled sword had teeth on one side of the blade as large as Riot's own hand.

The Trilords behind the queen each carried a thick, wooden pole.

"We heard you could use a hand," Queen Revna

said, brushing her long, white dreadlocks to the side. "Where do you want us?"

While the queen asked Riot where to be positioned, her warriors stationed the poles they carried against the wooden doors. One end rested on the thick wood, the other end was wedged into the dirt ground.

"We could use you here," Riot said, relieved. For the moment, it seemed the gate was safe. "I don't know how long Muscles—I mean, Prince Ketrick, will be able to hold them back with the dragon fire."

The queen nodded with a smile as if she knew what Riot had been about to say. Her eyes roved over the Marines, as well as Evonne with her skin coming off of her face. "Do your soldiers need medical attention?"

"What?" Riot looked from the queen to Evonne. "Oh no, she's fine."

"Does she have leprosy?" the queen asked, peering through the dark.

"No, no, nothing like that," Riot said, reminding herself it was still dark, and although her heads-up display brightened her vision, the same could not be said for everyone. "She's a Termina—ugh, Artificial Intelligence."

The queen looked at her, confused.

"She's a robot, as in 'not human,'" Doctor Miller said, trying to help. "She's part of our ship, the *Valkyrie*. She wanted a human-looking body, so Corporal Vetash and I created a frame for her and covered it with synthetic skin."

Queen Revna blinked a few times at Doctor Miller, then turned to Riot. "I think the doctor has received trauma to her head somewhere in today's conflict."

"You would think that, wouldn't you?" Riot said, nodding along with the queen's words. "I wonder the same thing about her myself on a daily basis."

"I'm right here." Doctor Miller placed closed fists on either side of her hips. "I can hear everything you're saying about me."

Riot, the queen, and everyone else had been complacent with having the playful banter, due to the fact that there was no main threat to the gate. Ketrick had his dragons performing alternate passes right in front of the gate. Every time a dragon swooped down, a thick flame of orange, red, and yellow fire erupted from their throats.

The Abomination horde fired their weapons at the dragons, but most of the shots either missed entirely or glanced off the dragons without inflicting even the tiniest bit of damage.

Dragon scales were impervious to small-weapons fire. Even the enemy fire from the Karnayer Scarabs were mostly ignored by the dragons. Along with the fire coming from the weapons and the hum emitted by the Abominations, a new sound began to fill the air.

Maybe it wasn't a sound at all. Perhaps it was a feeling. Whatever it was, Riot's sixth sense picked up on something approaching. She looked into the sky, seeing the twin suns of the planet beginning to rise over the horizon.

Riot switched off her helmet's heads-up display, allowing her to see what everyone else was looking at. She wasn't the only one to sense the feeling of trepidation. From far off, a massive shadow covered the sky. Riot squinted to try to see what it was.

"Do you hear something?" Killa asked over the comms. "Something in the jungle?"

"No, it's something in the sky," Colonel Harlan said over the comms. His voice sounded stressed. He was never stressed. "I'm getting word from Admiral Tricon and General Armon. The Karnayer destroyer has lowered back into orbit. The Scarabs are out in force. They're preparing their attack run."

"No, that's not it," Killa said, insistent, over the comms. "There's something else, something big coming from deep within the jungle's southern wall."

In that moment, something tickled the back of Riot's mind, some detail her subliminal consciousness had picked up on while she had somehow managed to forget.

"The smoke coming from the Karnayer drop ships," Riot said in a whisper to herself. Her voice was so low, no one else picked up on it over the nanites that allowed her to communicate even without her helmet.

Images of the smoke coming from the interior of the drop ships flashed across her mind. The sounds of Karnayer smiths working hard at their craft creating ...

what? Creating more Abominations, or something worse?

Riot was momentarily taken away from her thoughts as the Grovothe *Dreadnaught* and the *U.S.S. Patton* appeared over the Trilord city from their position in orbit and moved in to intercept the Karnayer destroyer.

Witnessing the crafts in the sky sail toward one another was like watching two massive bulls charging at one another. That is, if bulls weighed millions of tons and were equipped to the teeth with rail guns and laser weapons.

Riot ripped her thoughts from the sight of the colossal ships about to engage high in the sky, to an idea she understood was fact. How she knew, she wasn't sure, but she knew, nevertheless. "Killa, the Karnayers are going to throw everything at us now. They're engaging our fleet, not so they can win, but so that our ships will be unable to help us on the ground. The Karnayers are about to bring everything, including their own troops and their repurposed monsters."

"What are you talking about, Riot?" Colonel Harlan asked.

"The Karnayer drop ships in the jungle were hard at work making something and I didn't know what, until now. They were making wings, maybe armor, for their monsters. They knew Ketrick and the dragons would be able to stand against their ground forces," Riot said, explaining all of this, despite the fact she had no solid proof of her statements.

"How do you know this?" Killa asked.

"Because it's what I would do," Riot said, remembering the hate in Alveric's eyes. "Because it's what he would do."

A scream tore through the air at that moment, solidifying everything Riot had said up to that point. She had heard the sound before, but not on this planet. Riot ran up the stairs to the wall once more, and what she saw turned the blood in her veins to ice.

26

R iot crested the last step on the wall, looking out into the morning light covering the planet. Below her blazed a wall of flame nearly as tall as the wall itself. Just inside, stood Rippa and Atlas in their mechs.

Coming from the jungle interior were creatures Riot had seen before. Zenoth hive queens resurrected from the dead by a mixture of magic and machine. The insect-like monsters lumbered toward them.

That wasn't even the worst part. It seemed the Karnayer drop ships had been hard at work creating not just one of the terrifying beasts, but seven of the monstrosities.

Distant booms and bangs from far overhead reached Riot's ears, but in the moment, all she could concentrate on was the impossible freaks of science and magic in front of her.

"I've either done way too many drugs in my day, or I'm seeing seven Zenoth queens," Wang said from beside Riot. "Tell me you're seeing the same thing."

"You have done way too many drugs in your day," Riot said in answer, "but I'm seeing the same thing. Ketrick, if you can hear me, you need to break off protecting the gate and deal with the Zenoth queens."

"I see them," Ketrick said, bringing Vikta into a hovering position beside Riot on the wall. "I can deal with them, but that will leave the city without support. It's exactly what the Karnayers want."

"And we have to do it." Riot looked up to her right, where Ketrick sat on Vikta's wide back. The wind created by Vikta's giant wings pushed against her. "We'll hold the gate. You deal with the freaks. This has to be their final push."

"Vikta says to take care of yourself," Ketrick said over the comms. "She doesn't want to live in a universe without you."

Riot felt a giddy sensation rise in the pit of her stomach and spread across her entire body. The feeling didn't belong on a battlefield, but it was what she felt when Ketrick spoke to her about "Vikta's" feelings.

"I'll be fine, Vikta." Riot looked past the dragon's head to Ketrick. "You do the same. We have plans when this is all over."

Without another word, Ketrick took the dragons high into an arc where they would be better suited to descend upon the Zenoth hive queens.

"Wow, I never realized you and Vikta we're so close," Doctor Miller said in a serious tone. "That's great. A bond between a Marine and an alien dragon. That's a really beautiful thing, Riot. It gives me hope for the future."

Everyone looked over at Doctor Miller in disbelief.

Rizzo actually removed his helmet to give the doctor a deadpan stare.

"What? What did I miss?" Doctor Miller said. Even the Grovothe shock troops looked at her, shaking their heads.

"We have massive beasts coming from the jungle," Killa reported as the sounds of weaponsfire intensified from the south wall. "Hefty aliens walking on all fours with blasters on their backs, firing green energy. Five of them in total."

At the same time as Killa's report came in, the familiar wail of a Devil's Hand drifted over the south wall. Not just one voice, but multiple whale-like cries penetrated the Trilord city.

"Those are Devil's Hands," Riot said, already making up her mind on what had to be done. They couldn't afford to have the monsters' strange cries resurrecting the dead. "Ketrick, you have to go and take them out. You know you do. Go!"

"I—" Ketrick said.

The single word coming from Ketrick said it all; the hesitancy, the way he already was taking his dragons in a swing to the right.

"I'll be right back," Ketrick said through a clenched jaw. "Hold here, Sorceress. I'll only be a few minutes."

As soon as the dragons shifted to the right, the Zenoth hive queens charged. Not only them, but also the rest of the Abominations that still numbered in the thousands and a new addition to the battle—actual Karnayer troops dressed in their all-black armor and carrying high-powered blasters.

"Protect the gates!" Riot screamed into her comms. Her brain was working on overdrive as she witnessed the seven Zenoth hive queens spread their metal wings and soar low over the ground toward the gates. "Rippa, Atlas, focus fire on a single queen. Brimley, tell me you're locked and loaded."

"I'm ready," Brimley said over the comms.

"Great. Don't spread your fire. Just take a single queen down, then move on to the next," Riot said. She unhooked the warhammer from her back as the enemy closed.

Already the fire barriers from Ketrick's dragons were beginning to fade. Where once they had risen nearly two stories into the air, they now blazed no higher than Riot's five-foot-eight frame.

The main Karnayer force was still two hundred yards away and closing. Riot had precious few seconds to dole out orders that could very well decide the fate of the battle.

Her eyes focused on a crate of what looked like Grovothe grenades in a small box at her feet. A plan churned in Riot's mind as she shouted orders to the forces around her.

"Queen Revna, I need you and your warriors to hold the gates when they break through. I'm as optimistic as the next space Marine, but let's call a poodle a poodle, here," Riot said grabbing an armload of grenades. "I need some tape. Does anyone have tape?"

"Tape?" Wang repeated. "Why would anyone in a battle have tape?"

"Here." Doctor Miller reached Riot with a roll of black duct tape.

"Oh, of course she has some," Wang said, shaking his head. "So, next question: Why do you need tape?"

"Remember Afghanistan?" Riot asked, going to one knee. She wrapped as many grenades as she could around the head of her hammer. It wasn't pretty, but the grenades circled it like a ring around a planet.

Not Afghanistan, Rizzo typed over the screens in everyone's heads-up displays.

"Well, we have to die sooner or later," Vet said, joining Riot. He brought his sniper rifle from his back and began doing the same thing. He strapped grenade after grenade to the barrel of his weapon. "I guess this is as good as a time as any."

Wang and Rizzo joined in.

"Is someone going to explain to me what we're doing?" Doctor Miller looked on, perplexed. "They're about to reach the gates."

The familiar sounds of Rippa's and Atlas's mechs opening fire on the charging Zenoth queens filled the air.

VRRRROOOOOOOOM!

Brimley let her second and last salvo of rockets loose from their berths.

"Evonne, Cupcake, hold the gates at all costs," Riot ordered. "And pray the nanites work as well as we all hope they do."

"Epinephrine shots, anyone?" Wang stood up, holding the barrel of his Villain Pulse Rifle. Along the stock were duct-taped a glob of grenades. "I think Riot still has two, but I have more party favors for whoever wants some."

Riot was reminded she did, in fact, have two of the altered epinephrine pens in a side compartment in the lefthand side of her armored leg.

"No time." Riot looked to the charging Zenoth queens who were now less than a hundred yards from the gate. "Spread out across the wall, and whatever you do, don't miss."

"Oohrah!" Vet and Wang said in unison while Rizzo slammed a fist into his chest.

Riot backed up from the waist-high wall, preparing herself for what she was about to do next. She ran through the plans in her mind's eye, seeing her actions before she actually committed to them in real life.

Rippa's and Atlas's mechs were in bad condition from the waist down. The Abominations that had reached them with blades for hands had done a number on the outside of their armor. The left leg on Rippa's mech sparked, and with every movement, a huge portion of the armor had been ripped away to expose hoses and cords.

Atlas's mech wasn't any better. He was down on one knee. A small fire had broken out on the right leg of his mech near the ankle.

Both of the Grovothe pilots fought on despite their injuries. As one, they zeroed in on the same Zenoth queen flying toward the gate. In seconds, they had cut through its wings. They were now finishing off the freak of science-magic with a series of long laser blasts to the monster's head region.

Brimley's fire hammered a second giant Zenoth creature in the torso and skull as it stumbled and fell from the sky. That left five, closing in fast.

"Oohrah, Marines!" Riot yelled into the comms. "If I don't see you in this life again, I'll welcome you in the next!"

Riot heard their responses, but she was already moving toward her target. She was able to take two steps before her third landed her with her foot on the wall. She launched herself off the partition and sailed through the air at the same time she brought her warhammer in a wide swing.

Her timing had to be perfect for this to work. For a moment, she thought she had jumped too soon. The lead Zenoth queen she had chosen as her target still seemed too far away. Riot hung in the air as time slowed. Blue blaster fire erupted behind her as green return fire came at her from below.

Riot could see the Zenoth queen, up close and personal. It was the same kind of massive insect she had encountered before on the planet of Raydon. It looked like a giant praying mantis with multiple arms, huge eyes, pincers, and a row of sharp teeth.

Unlike before, this creature now had unnatural metal wings. A green glow came from its enormous eyes, and the arms on the right section of its body, along with a portion of its torso, were also metal.

Riot's last thoughts were on Ketrick as a roar built deep in her chest.

I wonder what life we could have had together, Riot thought as time began to speed up. *I'll see you again one day.*

As if time were trying to make up for its temporary lapse, the next second sped by.

"Rawww!" Riot screamed as her warhammer strapped with grenades came down on the Zenoth queen's head.

It was a perfect blow. Riot hit the queen with every ounce of strength she could muster. At the same time she pressed the trigger on her weapon.

BAM!

The last thing Riot remembered was a bright light as she was hurled back into the air like a rock thrown from a catapult.

27

R iot didn't drink anymore, but the events that occurred now reminded her of times before when she would black in and out of unconsciousness. It was like she was getting snapshots of what was happening to her instead of the full movie.

No pain, only a numb sensation raced across her body. She was flying through the air in an upward arc.

Things faded to black.

Riot slammed into the ground, where an explosion of pain erupted in her head. The wind was not just knocked out of her, it was sucked out of her lungs as if from a vacuum hose.

She couldn't move.

Riot opened her eyes, trying in vain to make sense of what had happened. Half of her helmet was gone, along with parts of her armor. Although her armor had absorbed a portion of the explosion, it had not been able to keep her safe. The impact of the grenades detonating at that close a range meant her armor had been torn open at the chest.

Riot was lying on her left side. She managed to look down. Her chest was a mess of blood and open flesh. Breathing came hard. There was something wrong with her left eye.

"Well, well, well," Alveric's voice said from somewhere above her. "What do we have here?"

Riot still couldn't move. At the moment, breathing was hard enough. She was able to look up at Alveric, who was surrounded by a contingent of Karnayer soldiers.

As much as she wanted to tell him he looked like she felt, her lips wouldn't move.

"I would kill you now. I could kill you now." Alveric lifted a curved sword from a sheath at his side. He pressed the tip against the bottom of Riot's chin where her helmet had been blown away. "But I'd rather have you watch the city burn as you die."

Alveric laughed as the sword's razor sharp edge broke into Riot's skin and brought her head up to look at the city. The sword dug a bright red trench into her cheek.

Riot knew she should be feeling the pain of the cut, but it seemed her system was still in some kind of deep-seated shock. Instead of the pain, she focused on what she was seeing. Her trajectory after the explosion had sent her up and back down the long road that led to the Trilord city. She was now looking up the dirt road to the city, about fifty yards from the gates.

Smoking corpses of all of the Zenoth queens lay along the road to the gates. All but one had been killed by either her Marines or the Grovothe mechs. There was no sign of her War Wolves. Rippa's and Atlas's mechs were both down. The only mech still operating was the fortress class Brimley occupied. Its Gatling gun-like arms still firing at the single remaining Zenoth queen who battered at the gates.

Alveric laughed again, then continued on to the city.

Behind the Zenoth queen striking the gates was an army of Abomination and Karnayer soldiers.

Riot coughed blood as the nanites in her body struggled to keep her alive long past the time she should have already died. The comms in Riot's helmet were beyond repair. At the moment, she didn't even know if she had it in her to try to contact anyone else with the nanites that connected her to the rest of the crew.

Get up. You have to get up, Riot thought. *If you can't do it for yourself, do it for them. Do it for him.*

With a loud crack, the gates to the Trilord city finally broke. A cheer went up from the Karnayer soldiers as they allowed the Abomination force to stream inside.

Riot could hear the fire of Trilord weapons as

Queen Revna and her dragon-tattooed warriors tried to hold the gate.

They can't hold the gate by themselves, not for long, Riot thought. *Get up! Get up! You have to get up!*

Riot moved her right hand first, and then her left. The pain came from her ripped-open chest more than from anywhere else. Other areas of her body screamed to be heard, but they paled in comparison to the fire she felt in her lungs.

Clawing her way through the dirt road, Riot made use of her hands first, then began trying to move her feet. She made it to her knees. She sat back on them, trying to gather herself. The only good news at the moment was that the Trilords and the forces gathered in the city were still holding the enemy in the entrance to the gate. The fighting had turned from blasters to hand-to-hand combat.

Riot's left hand slid down from her lap to the compartment on her leg where her two last epinephrine shots still rested.

I wonder what will happen if I take two, Riot thought. *There's only one way to find out.*

Riot opened the compartment in her armor, grateful it had been an area that had escaped the initial blast. She ignored the multiple open wounds on her body still oozing dark red blood. She opened up the lids on both pens and, without giving her actions a second thought, plunged them into the side of her neck. In one move, she pressed down both plungers.

"Ugh, this was a mistake," Riot managed to finally groan as lightning raced through her veins. "Ahh!"

Riot's body was alive with energy unlike anything she had ever experienced before. Her hands shook, her body quivered with so much force she thought she was going to have a seizure. Then, immediately, her mind cleared and her vision came back as if the epinephrine shots had given the nanites in her body the boost they needed to speed up repairs.

Riot got to her feet and began to walk up the dirt road.

"Alveric," Riot said, at first unable to bring her voice much over a whisper. There must have been extensive damage to her mouth and throat that the nanites would have to repair before she could say anything. "Alveric."

The enemy forces had their backs toward her. The battle still raged just inside the city gate. The giant Zenoth queen's head barely touched the top of the arched gateway. Someone on the other side was managing to keep her at bay. On all sides of the archway, the enemy tried to enter, like an ocean of enemies waiting for the dam to break, and flow through the open gates.

"Alveric!" Riot said, louder this time. She wasn't able to run yet, but she was feeling stronger. "Alveric!"

She saw him standing at the edge of his army, staying at the rear of his men like a true leader.

"Alveric!" Riot screamed, the energy coursing through her body reaching a point where she felt as though she might be able to run. "Hey, you blue-skinned, elf-looking mother gunner. I'm talking to you!"

Alveric finally turned. The look on his face was priceless—one part wonder, one part fear.

Riot started to run the last few yards to Alveric and his group of personal guards. She reached down, grabbing one of the Karnayer rifles fallen from some dead soldier already forgotten.

Still running, Riot aimed down the barrel.

Four shots and four hits took out Alveric's guards. He reached for his blade. Riot zeroed in on a head shot and pressed the trigger. A click told her she was empty.

Riot slammed into Alveric instead, using the rifle like a club.

The two combatants went down hard. Riot abandoned the hold on her own weapon for the hilt on Alveric's sword. She remembered her battle with Remus and how the Karnayer blades worked. Their edges covered in a bright sheen of green magic were capable of cutting through any other material like a laser through ice.

Riot and Alveric rolled on the dirt ground, each trying to rip the grip of the sword hilt from one another's hands. If the Marines had taught Riot anything, it was how to ignore pain and that little voice in your head that insisted you couldn't. Instead of giving into self doubt, Riot fought on, ignoring all the reasons why she was too weak to win this fight.

The two combatants finally rolled to a standstill on the dirt road. Alveric was on top of her. He leveraged his entire body to bear down, trying to drive the long blade into her neck.

The sword had been wrestled in a parallel position. The edge of the blade was mere inches from Riot's throat. Riot's broken helmet had come off completely as the two combatants rolled on the ground. She could see her own reflection in the mirror of the green blade.

Her face was still a ruin of blood and torn skin that was already repairing itself, thanks to the nanites coursing through her veins.

"Why won't you just die?" Alveric spat through gritted teeth. His blue skin and white hair were stained with dirt, a gleam of sweat gathered on his brow. "Give in. Give in to the death waiting for you."

Riot's hands were shaking. Where Alveric had the entire weight of his body to use to push the blade down, Riot only had her arms as if she were using a bench press machine. She understood she had moments left before her strength gave out.

Anger burned inside of Riot. Anger, not only for her, but also for all the other alien species Alveric and the Karnayers like him had enslaved. With one last effort, Riot managed to roll to her left and fling the blade to the side.

Alveric countered by releasing his hold on the blade, allowing it to fall. Instead of losing his top position, he began to rain down blows across Riot's head and face.

Stars exploded across Riot's vision for the second time that day. The pain, Riot could deal with. What she was really worried about was being knocked unconscious before she could finally kill the alien bully on top of her.

Riot threw a few punches of her own, landing them across Alveric's jaw and nose. Blood poured from both of his own nostrils and a split lip.

"Enough!" Alveric screamed, reaching for a long blade hidden in his belt. "Now you die!"

A thought so insane crossed Riot's mind that it made her smile.

"Why are you smiling?" Alveric demanded. He lifted the blade above his head in both of his hands to drive down into Riot.

"You'll see," Riot said.

Alveric screamed as he pushed the blade down.

Instead of doing what he thought she would by lifting her hands to stop the blade, Riot moved to the side, allowing the green knife-edge to enter her left shoulder as opposed to the area over her heart. Doing this meant two things happened.

First, pain. So much pain, Riot thought for sure she would pass out. A fiery sensation started at her shoulder and spread outward as if heat were actually spreading across her body.

Second, by Alveric committing his entire strength to the stabbing motion, his head had bowed down close enough for Riot to grab. Riot reached up, clutched Alveric around the throat with both hands and, with everything she had, she squeezed.

A look of utter panic took hold of Alveric as all sense lost him. Instead of trying to take the blade out of Riot and stab her again, his hands immediately traveled to his throat to try to pry off her merciless fingers.

"You messed with the wrong species this time," Riot said as she found Alveric's windpipe below his folds of skin and tore this section of his throat from his neck.

Alveric gasped as blue blood pooled down his neck and onto his black clothes. Both of his hands struggled to hold the wound closed as more and more lifeblood pooled out. He fell to his side, choking on his own plasma.

Riot struggled to her feet. The blade still in her shoulder sent a stab of pain through her fatigued body. She reached for the fallen sword by Alveric and lifted it over the alien.

"You—all of you—will die," Alveric managed to choke out.

"Maybe." Riot lifted the sword over her head. "But not today."

Riot drove the sword down, splitting Alveric's head like an overripe watermelon. As soon as she had performed the action, she knew it was the last thing she was able to do before her body gave in to her wounds. Nanites or not, she had taken on too much damage.

Riot sank to her knees.

Everything went dark.

28

Riot wasn't sure if she was dreaming, or if she had died and this is what the afterlife had waiting for her. She was lying in a white bed with clean, fluffy sheets and pillows surrounding her.

There was no pain in her body, but an exhaustion she had never experienced before lay across her frame.

It was only when she sat up to study the room she realized she wasn't alone. Queen Revna was dressed in a white gown. Her dark skin was free of any scars or wounds. Her white hair seemed to glow all on its own.

"Calm down, Riot." Queen Revna smiled. "You're not the one who's dead."

Riot had a hard time processing the queen's words. When she did, a ball of angst grew in the pit of her stomach.

"The battle ... I killed Alveric, I—" Riot tried to

make sense of what was happening. "You were at the gate."

"I was." The queen traveled to the side of Riot's bed and took a seat. "I fought alongside humans and Grovothe alike, and we held the gate. After the sacrifice you and your Marines made against the giant insect creatures, everyone rallied to hold the city. I died there, taking down the last insect beast, and I wouldn't have it any other way. I died in service for my people and our alliance."

"I'm sorry … I'm really sorry. I've been blown up, stabbed, and hit in the head too many times today," Riot said, blinking and shaking her head. "Did you say you died?"

"Yes," the queen said with a smile that was devoid of any sadness. "I don't have much time left. They're strict about the rules here. I just wanted to come to you and tell you that when you wake up, he'll need you. He acts like a stone, but inside, his heart beats like our own."

Riot didn't even have to ask who the queen was talking about. She understood now the queen had come back from the dead to give her a final message about her son.

"He'll be king now, and he'll need a queen to rule at his side." Queen Revna eyed Riot with a sly smile. "I've seen how you two are together."

"Hey, I don't have any desire to be queen of anything," Riot said, again shaking her head.

"The best queens never do." Revna took Riot's hand

into her own. "Just promise me you'll look after him. That will be enough."

"I will. Of course I will," Riot said, holding the queen's hands tightly in her own. "I promise."

"And give me a lot of human-Trilord grandbabies," the queen added in a rush of words as she stood from the bed and made for the door.

"What?!" Riot cried, half-getting out of the bed. "I didn't agree to that. That wasn't part of our deal!"

Everything faded to a bright white. The last thing Riot remembered was the same genuine smile on the queen's lips as she walked out of the room.

Riot blinked multiple times, trying to make sense of what she had just seen and where she was now. Gone were all the white sheets and the fluffy, clean bed. Riot lay in the middle of the road where she had killed Alveric. In fact, his corpse was still lying beside her. From her view on her back, Riot looked into the clear morning sky.

"Riot! Riot!" Someone was yelling in the distance. "Riot, where are you!?"

"She would be the one to find me," Riot said out loud as she remained lying down, but titled her head up to see Doctor Miller racing toward her. "Just my luck."

"Riot!" Doctor Miller sprinted to her side. She came to one knee beside Riot, looking down at her. She took off her helmet to reveal a face full of concern. "What did you say? Did you say something?

Riot! Riot, talk to me. I'm here for you. You're not alone."

"I said I'm happy to see you," Riot lied.

"Oh, you're alive!" Doctor Miller wrapped Riot into a hug and squeezed so hard, Riot thought the doctor was going to finish the job Alveric had started.

"Easy," Riot said in a high-pitched voice. "I can't breathe."

"Oh, oh right." Doctor Miller released Riot. She was crying. "I'm just … I just thought I lost you."

Riot looked up at Doctor Miller. Her tears were so genuine, her sadness so real, it struck a chord somewhere deep within Riot. She felt her own eyes tingle and burn with the beginnings of tears.

"No. No way." Riot shook her head. "I'm not crying with you. Help me up, Cupcake."

Doctor Miller reached down to obey and hefted Riot into a sitting position.

For the first time since she had woken, Riot noticed that the sounds of war had vanished. Silence, maybe a few distant voices, were the only things that could be heard now.

"What happened?" Riot asked while she tried out her various limbs, a question she already knew the answer to as memories of the queen's visit cascaded into her thoughts. "Did we win?"

"We won," Doctor Miller said, pointing to Riot's shoulder. "Is that … is that a knife sticking out of you? Want me to take it out?"

Riot looked down to see the handle of Alveric's knife still in her body.

"That would probably be a good thing," Riot said, gritting her teeth.

"Okay, here we go—one ... one and a half ... two ... two and a half..."

"For all that is holy, will you please—"

Doctor Miller tore the blade from Riot's shoulder. The pain that came with the act was like ripping off a scab still in the process of healing.

Riot's face must have betrayed her emotions, because Doctor Miller took a step back.

"Sorry, I read in an article that if your patient is—"

"Can it, Bubbles." Riot lifted a hand to the doctor. "Help me get up and tell me what happened."

Doctor Miller obeyed, lifting Riot to her feet. "We were holding the gate, but just barely. Queen Revna went down fighting the last Zenoth hive queen. She and Evonne were the ones who'd finally brought it down. It was hell at the gates, the Abomination horde slicing and the Karnayer army shooting like crazy, trying to get in. I thought we were going to be overrun, when the Abominations suddenly just dropped."

"What?" Riot asked her. "How?"

"I don't know." Doctor Miller shrugged. One second we were all fighting for our lives; and the next, the Abominations dropped dead. The lights in their green eyes went out. It was like someone had killed their power supply or whoever it was controlling them.

After that, the Karnayer soldiers still standing ran. Same with the Karnayer ships battling it out in the sky."

Riot turned back to look at the city gates that lay broken. Portions of the wall were on fire. Other sections had been blasted to splinters. Rippa's and Atlas's mech lay on the ground around piles of enemy soldiers.

"Where are the others? How long has the fight been over?"

"Not more than twenty minutes," Doctor Miller said, opening her hands in front of her. "And the others are all okay, too. Wang, Rizzo, and Vet all made it back after their explosions. Wang has a hearing problem now, but I think that's just until the nanites repair the damage to his inner ear."

Riot took a tentative step forward, back up the dirt road. When she found she wasn't in danger of falling, she took another and another.

"Where's Ketrick?" Riot asked, already thinking of the man she loved. "Does he know about his mother yet?"

"No, I don't think so." Doctor Miller walked beside Riot. "Are the communication nanites fried?"

"I think so," Riot said, still unable to hear anything from the outside comms. Even her link to Evonne seemed to be down. "Evonne, are you reading me? Evonne?"

Nothing.

"Still down," Riot said, walking back up the road to the burning city gates.

As they approached the city, the carnage they walked over made Riot shudder. She had no problem killing when killing was the only way, but the amount of bodies littering the ground was nauseating. Thousands of Abomination soldiers, either dead by their own hands or fallen inactive when Alveric was taken out, lined the road.

It soon became so bad, Riot and Doctor Miller couldn't walk without stepping on the dead bodies. Here and there, a Karnayer soldier lay still, but the vast majority of the corpses belonged to the Abomination horde.

The two giant mech warriors Rippa and Atlas had used in the fight both lay on either side of the gates, like two fallen sentries having given up their final claim on the world.

Riot looked up into the bright sky to see both the *Dreadnaught* and the *U.S.S. Patton* drifting back their way. They were too far away to see what general state of disrepair the ships were in, but the fact they were still flying was a good sign.

As Riot and Doctor Miller walked between the hulking fallen mechs, shouts came from the wall. Cheers erupted from all those still standing. Vet, Wang, and Rizzo all ran to see Riot. The three Marines were safe, but sections of their armor had been either blown off or torn off.

Vet approached with both hands on his helmet, placed over his groin.

"Man, am I glad to see you," Vet said to Riot with a smile as she entered what was left of the gate. "I thought for a second you'd taken your final ride."

I knew you were too stubborn to go out like that, Rizzo signed. He pointed to Vet's helmet. *The XO had a wardrobe malfunction.*

"You're alive!" Wang shouted so loud, everyone in the vicinity gave them their attention. He pushed a finger into his ear as if that would help his hearing. "Have you seen Vet!? He swears he's still in one piece down there, but I don't know! I don't want to look!"

Riot rolled her eyes, yet couldn't help smiling. To her left, she caught sight of Rippa and Atlas having their wounds patched up by a Grovothe medic.

Inside the walls and to the right of the gate, the remaining Trilords had lain Queen Revna's body on a clean, white blanket. She wore the same peaceful smile on her lips Riot had remembered in her dream.

What am I going to say to him? Riot thought as she considered the words she would need when Ketrick arrived. *How can I take away any of the pain he's about to feel?*

Riot wished she had come up with a plan before the rush of wings signaling Ketrick's return sounded overhead.

29

Ketrick touched down on Vikta a few moments later. Whether he knew something was wrong because he had been warned, or just sensed it, Riot wasn't sure.

The Trilord Prince jumped off Vikta's back before the dragon had come to a complete stop. He ran to Riot and wrapped her in a hug. It didn't matter to him who was watching at the moment.

Riot hesitated for a moment, but only for a moment. The universe was changing, and she could, too. She grabbed on to Ketrick tight, lost in his huge arms. The Trilord prince had sustained his own injuries. Black streaks of smoke covered his body, while dried blood told stories all their own.

"I'm so happy you're safe," Ketrick said, burying his head into her shoulder. "I heard confused messages over the comms and wasn't sure what happened. I came as fast as I could."

The same fear of not knowing what to say took hold of Riot's gut. Ketrick didn't know about his mother. He had flown back and seemed in such a hurry for her.

"Ketrick." Riot pushed him gently back and told him how she would want to be told. No beating around the bush; just the truth, however harsh it may be. "Your mother, the queen ... she didn't make it. She died defending the city."

Ketrick's eyebrows furrowed in confusion. He looked up, searching the smoking battlefield for his mother. His Adam's apple bobbed up and down as he swallowed hard.

Tears filled his eyes as he searched for someone he knew he would never see alive again. "Where ... where is she?"

"Here, here." Riot took his hand and led him to the spot where the other Trilords had gathered.

As soon as the other Trilord warriors saw who approached, they went down to one knee. Not a single eye was dry amongst the gathered group of ferocious warriors.

Tears fell freely from Ketrick's eyes as he looked down at his mother. He took one of her hands into his own and fell to his knees. Although tears washed down his cheeks, no whimpers or cries escaped his throat.

Riot felt hot tears gathering in her own eyes as she

looked on. What was she supposed to say? What could she say?

Ketrick leaned over and kissed his mother's forehead. He stood back, laying her hand gently by her side.

"She … she would have … she would have wanted to die like this," Ketrick finally managed. "She was … a warrior before a queen."

Riot gathered Ketrick into her arms as if he were shorter than she. In that moment, he fit into her embrace like a small child. Riot didn't have to say anything. Ketrick cried into her shoulder for a moment. Brief deep tremors shook his shoulders.

Riot held him so hard that, had he been anyone else, she would have been afraid she might crush them.

A moment later, Ketrick pulled away. If he was ashamed for everyone to see the tears spilling down his face, he didn't show it.

Every Trilord warrior present remained on their knees to pay respect to their new king.

* * *

"So you ripped out his throat, huh?" General Armon looked over to Riot with a twitch of his lips. "That sounds like something you would do."

Riot stood beside the general on their spot next to the capitol building. From this vantage, they could look out over the city, or what was left of it. The fires that had once run unopposed in the city had been put out. The dead belonging to them were being prepared for burial, while the enemy corpses were being burned.

Riot looked over to her left where, just down the hill, Ketrick, her War Wolves, and Rippa were all taking a brief moment to express their gratefulness for each other having lived through the engagement. Ketrick even went so far as to pat Rippa on the shoulder. Rippa nearly stumbled back from the act.

"It's not over, is it?" Riot asked herself more than the general standing beside her. "It'll never be over."

"Planets, people, aliens will always need to be protected," General Armon said, catching Riot's eye. "The universe is a sandbox with bullies in it, just like anywhere else."

"General, I think I may need a br—"

"It's come to my attention that you and your crew more than deserve a much-needed rest," General Armon said, interrupting Riot before she could continue. "You know our position, though, so I can't give you a break, can I?"

"I understand," Riot said, licking her dry lips. Was she really going to ask for a leave of absence now? Could she, when there was still so much to do? "General, maybe—"

"But what I can do," the general interrupted again. His eyes told her he knew exactly what she was going to request. "I can assign you to remain here on Hoydren. I'm calling Colonel Harlan and his team back to Earth. They'll soon leave to be the emissaries between the Grovothe and SPEAR. I couldn't think of a better person to leave here to help the Trilords rebuild than you and your team."

"Thank you," Riot said to the general. He had given her exactly what she wanted without her even having to ask for a break. She was a Marine, and Marines didn't need breaks. But this time of rest wouldn't be for her, it would be to keep a promise she had made to a queen. Although, if she was being truly honest with herself, it was a little bit for her.

Laughter, despite the hour, rose up from the group of warriors to her left. Vet or Wang had said something funny, and Rippa, as well as Ketrick, was bent over laughing. Rizzo was shaking his head, while Doctor Miller tried to explain to Evonne what was so funny.

"Use this time to rest and help the Trilords build." General Armon's voice was stern. "The fight is far from over."

"Oohrah, sir," Riot said, saluting her superior officer.

"Oohrah, Marine." The general saluted her back.

Riot reminded herself to walk, not run, back to her team, her family. As she got closer, she picked up on Vet's voice and the story he was telling.

"And I see Doctor Miller, there, all wide-eyed and sweating, and she's hitting this Abomination over and over and over again. I mean, this thing isn't moving, and its guts are just plastered all over the ground. I think Rippa's mech had stomped it already," Vet said, pausing to laugh. "And I come up, and I'm like: Doc, I think it's dead."

"In my defense, I'm not a warrior, like you guys are." Doctor Miller shook her head with a good-natured smile of her own. "I didn't know if it was going to get up and try to shank me or something."

"Shank you?" Wang doubled over, laughing. "What are we, in prison or something? An Abomination would have stabbed you or blown you away."

"What does the word 'shank' mean?" Ketrick asked with a raised eyebrow.

"Here, let me show you," Rippa said, pulling a knife from a holster in her boot.

"You should really not be shanking one another," Evonne said as Rizzo plucked the knife out of Rippa's hand.

"What?" Rippa said and looked around with a shrug. "I wasn't going to shank him hard."

"All right, you misfits," Riot said, joining her family. "If anyone should be showing anyone how to shank someone, it should be me. Who wants to go first?"

THE END

ABOUT THE AUTHORS

Jonathan Yanez

Jonathan Yanez is the author of over a dozen fantasy and science fiction novels. His works include; The Elite Series, The Nephilim Chronicles, Thrive, Bad Land and The DeCadia Code. He has been both traditionally and independently published with his works being adapted into; ebook, print, audiobook and even optioned for film.

Although writing has been and will always be his main love, physical exercise comes in at a close second. When he's not writing his next novel that more than likely includes some kind of zombie, superhero, angel or alternative steampunk universe he enjoys running with his dogs and working out at the gym.

His hobbies include archery, mud runs, collecting the skulls of his enemies and baking cupcakes. He lives in Southern California with his wife and three pets where he stays highly caffeinated 24/7

http://www.jonathan-yanez.com
https://twitter.com/JonathanAYanez
http://www.facebook.com/JonathanYanezAuthor

Justin Sloan

After serving five years in Marine Corps Signals Intelligence, Justin studied fiction at the Johns Hopkins MA in writing program and screenwriting at UCLA. He went on to work in games and screenwriting, where he has optioned several screenplays and written on such games as Game of Thrones and Tales from the Borderlands.

Justin has presented on writing at the Austin Film Festival, San Francisco Writers Conference, the San

Diego State Writers Conference, Gen Con, and more. You can hear his interviews with authors on the Creative Writing Career podcast.

His books are available in audio and print editions, and he has sold Turkish and French rights to several of his series, with the Blade of the Sea series being published under Hachette Publishing Group (under the shared penname with PT Hylton of Jesse Nethermind).

Justin loves to hear from you, so please feel free to visit http://www.justinsloanauthor.com/seppukarian to join the email list, receive a free book, receive free giveaways, get the latest exclusive news, connect on Facebook and Twitter, and stay in touch!

www.JustinSloanAuthor.com
  Facebook: http://facebook.com/JustinSloanAuthor
  Twitter: http://twitter.com/justinmsloan
  Audible: http://adbl.co/1G4tbIy

WHAT NEXT?

Thank you for reading Light Em Up! **Please review Book 3 Today.**

* * *

For the Seppukarian Universe newsletter, join here.

Or to www.JustinSloanAuthor.com/Seppukarian.

***

This book is part of the Seppukarian Universe, though it stands on its own. If you would like to check out the other spinoff series, as listed in the SHIFTING DIMENSIONS anthology.

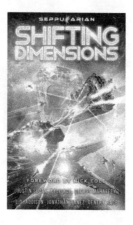

Marines think outside the box, but what happens when they think outside the known universe and time itself?

Whisked away through time loops that distort reality, a group of Space Marines explore different worlds and shifting dimensions as they combat an alien invasion. The edge-of-your-seat adventures in these alternative realities form the backbone of this anthology, which is full of exciting stories from debut and best-selling authors in the science fiction genre. Come aboard and experience exhilarating battles against mechs, drones, alien warriors with biotech armor, and tales of future combat that will blow your mind.

Featuring a Foreword by Nick Cole

Featured Authors:

 L.O. Addison

 George S. Mahaffey Jr.

 Kyle Noe

 Gentry Race

 Justin Sloan

 Jonathan Yanez

Grab it on Amazon

***

You can check out the Syndicate Wars books, if you want the backstory for these spinoffs and this anthology. They are like the prequels—you don't have to read them, but might have fun if you do. And the first three are coming out from Podium in an Audiobook boxset - November 28!

Grab it on Amazon

***

Justin Sloan released his first spinoff in the series as well! You can find **Shadow Corps** available online today:

Death isn't so bad if it means saving the universe.

Samantha was badass even before she learned magic. Fending for herself in the cauldron of a planet torn apart by an alien invasion taught Samantha how to kill. Ruthlessly efficient, her abilities have caught the attention of the Shadow Corps.

A group comprised of deadly warriors who focus on galactic safety, using any means necessary.

A battle-hardened warlord causing you trouble? The Shadow Corps will ruin their day.

Her first mission puts her team up against a space dragon, death reapers, and the ultimate sorcerer.

Samantha had better learn to master her alien magic, or be forced to watch her world, and many others, burn.

Grab it on Amazon

* * *

And here's a sample of Justin's SHADOW CORPS!

To ensure you don't miss future, head over to Justin's or Jonathan's Amazon pages and follow the authors.

SHADOW CORPS SAMPLE

The first time Samantha had seen the world end, it had terrified her.

Of course, that vision had been long ago. Over three years, if her estimation was correct. Since then, the vision had come to her in nightmares and flashes in her mind, and each time it seemed more blurred, more… unsure.

The vision was always the same—an alien armada unlike anything the world had ever seen. Not the invasion that had already taken over the world and held it in a state of martial law. No, this invasion would put their current overlords to shame. The Syndicate would fight and, in the end, be crushed.

It didn't help that others called her crazy.

It also didn't help that she was certain she would have a hand in saving the world, because that meant it could only end badly. Either she would be proven right, and an alien invasion greater than any they had ever known would destroy their world, or she would fulfill her destiny, but her so-called friends would go on thinking she was insane.

The latter would do, she decided as she stared out of her foxhole, waiting for the Syndicate drone to fly by. They always did at this time of day—a patrol, one of many set up to ensure everyone was in by curfew. If the drone was lucky, it would find members of the resistance, the Last Remaining Resistance, or LRR, as its members liked to refer to it.

There had once been a world with governments and their separate militaries, a Space Corps of Marines —and a resistance. That resistance had sometimes partnered with the Space Corps and other militaries, sometimes went out on their own, and sometimes even fought against the militaries. But not anymore. Now it was simply the LRR, a rag-tag group of survivors that had joined together when the Syndicate had won.

It all started with the day Samantha's mom, Quinn, went missing. But Samantha preferred not to think about that, especially not when such thoughts could distract her and ruin her chance of hitting her target.

Their goal today was simple—knock out the drones within a one-block radius, then hit the local patrol mech.

Ever since the Syndicate had won, cities were scoured by drones looking for trouble. If they found it, patrol mechs would come through to collect prisoners... or leave bodies.

Samantha's faction of the LRR had formulated a plan to secure a block, set up anti-air missiles and a defense against Syndicate air strikes, and then, if possible, take over one of the mechs. With Dan's hacking skills, Samantha almost believed it could be possible.

She smiled at the thought of Dan, with his piercing blue eyes like ice. Not the kind of ice that would freeze your heart, but the kind that stopped you dead in your tracks. Too bad he was six years her senior, a fact he didn't know, but bothered her.

A whirring sound came from nearby, and Samantha checked the display on her armband. It showed incoming blips that she took for at least three drones. More than she had expected, but not unmanageable.

She wrapped her arm in the sling of her rifle for stability, then sat cross-legged and formed a triangle with her arms, right finger on the trigger. Breathing in, she watched the sights rise slightly above the zone where she had spotted the drone pass the last three days in a row. Breathing out, the sights lined up perfectly.

The whirring grew louder. Her mind wandered to Dan again, imagining him down there, preparing his gear to make a move on the mech when it showed up. He was so diligent when he worked, so focused on the task and on achieving the goal. She smiled, remembering how they had met, him guarding her when she was imprisoned by a group of raiders and resistance.

How funny that now they were working together.

"Go time!" one of the women in the team, Ashley, whispered through the earpiece, pulling Sam back to the present.

Breathe in. Breathe out.

WHIRRRRR....

BAM!

She had squeezed the trigger, the bullet had hit its target, and down went the first drone.

Checking her screen, Samantha didn't see the other two. In fact, she saw nothing. This could mean the others weren't there at all, or it could mean their signals were being scrambled.

"Shit," she said into her earpiece. "Anyone there?"

No response. They were definitely being scrambled. That was bad.

Without hesitation, Samantha stood, turned back to the fire escape she had been camped out on, and ran up to the roof, ducking between the brick stairwell exit and a series of fans.

It was dangerous being out in the open, but she had to see what they were up against. She spotted Ashley on the next building over, under a tarp spray painted gray so it acted as camouflage from anyone above. The woman saw her too, gesturing for her to get back down.

Ashley held her hand to her ear and said something, but nothing came through. Ashley's face scrunched up, and she repeated herself. It was a look she wore too often—a look that seemed to say "Why are you so stupid?" A look that Samantha had more than once wanted to smack off that pretty face.

Maybe it had something to do with the fact that Ashley and Dan had been rumored to have feelings for each other, though there hadn't been any proof on the matter.

Wait a minute, Samantha realized. If Ashley didn't know the comms weren't working, maybe hers still were? And if only Samantha's weren't, that meant at least one of the drones was on her side of the building.

She threw caution to the wind and ran to the edge of the roof, staying low as best she could until she reached the ledge. She ducked and took a deep breath, then lifted her rifle and spun, aiming down, searching.

She spotted one.

BAM!

It fell, only to be replaced by another a moment later. This one had spotted Samantha immediately, and a red light flickered on at the drone's metallic nose.

"Shit shit shit!" Samantha said. Then, to her surprise, a click sounded in her earpiece.

"What'd you do, girl?" Ashley demanded, and Samantha realized taking out the one drone had canceled the interference.

BAM! She shot, and missed. Blasts flew out from

the drone, sending bits of the concrete barrier into the air as Sam ducked, pulling herself across the rooftop and back to cover.

The whirring grew louder, and she turned to see the drone rise over the ledge. It aimed in at her, and then—

BAM! Ashley had fired, clipping the drone's wing and causing its shot to barely miss Samantha.

The mech turned, did a quick scan of the area, and then retreated.

"It's pulling back until reinforcements arrive!" Samantha shouted, leaping to her feet and giving chase. "DAMMIT!"

She reached the ledge, put one foot on it to use her knee to stabilize her rifle, then fired. The shot made contact, causing the drone to veer to its left and then crash into the building.

But it was too late. The signal had been sent out and, when she looked at her screen, there were five or six more incoming. And something large.

"Guys, that mech is coming back, but it ain't alone."

"We see that," Ashley's voice responded, the electronics not failing to hide the irritation.

"Just stay sharp," Dan said. "I'm coming up."

"We need you down there," Ashley said. "That mech won't be ours if you don't do your job."

"And if you two die, we're in trouble."

Sam knew he was right. He would need all hands covering his ass while he hacked into the mech. And since the LRR had sent a team of only five, losing two would be a big loss.

"I got this," she said, this time standing and deliberately walking back toward the edge of the roof.

"No!" Ashley called out. "Not this again! Come on, someone get this whacko under control!"

"I can do it, I swear." The words caused her mouth to go dry. She had done it before, this magic. More than once, as a matter of fact. She'd had a teacher back then, a man who had shown her how to manipulate matter. To do *magic*, if you wanted to call it that. He didn't, though. He said it was simply science, learning how to connect with matter and change it to your will.

But she had been younger then, barely a teen. The memories were fading, and lately she had even started to wonder if the others were right, if it had all been a dream and she was a nut-job.

The man who called himself Gunny—nothing more, just Gunny—insisted in his insensitive way that she had "Gone ape-shit" the day her mom went missing. Others, including Dan, had heard about her exploits even before then, and speculated that she had gone crazy years before her mom's disappearance.

None of their accusations mattered to Sam, though. Sometimes at night she would wake up, feeling the power course through her. She would imagine that day her mom had left, as Dan had said it happened. She had likely believed Samantha to be dead, a thought that haunted those dreams more than any other.

Samantha had survived the explosion. She had saved her mom's life.

Wherever she fell on the spectrum between normal and bat-shit crazy, she was sure of those two things.

And right now she was going to put her powers to the test.

Feet planted firmly apart, she focused on her breathing. Deep breath in, slowly letting it out. *Focus.*

The whirring drew closer, nearly upon her. Ashley's cursing grew louder in her ear, until finally Samantha tore out the earpiece.

Again she focused on her breathing, but as the whirring grew louder she knew her heart was beating too fast, her palms were too clammy—it wasn't happening.

"Dammit, girl!" Dan shouted, appearing next to her with his plasma blaster at the ready.

The sight of those eyes staring at her would've made her weak in the knees, if not for the mix of ferocity and disappointment in them.

"I can do it," she insisted, knowing she was trying to convince herself as much as him.

He just shook his head, a compassion coming over his eyes that bordered on pity, and then turned to lift his blaster and fire.

Ashley appeared a moment later, blowing her cover to join in the defense of their rooftop, and soon it was clear their scanners had been dead wrong. There weren't just a few extra drones, there were at least a dozen.

Dan pulled Samantha back by the collar into the protection of the stairwell, then shouted for her to snap out of it.

She stared at the drones, hearing them fire and watching as bullets and lasers tore apart the roof nearby, and gathered her will. Shouldering her rifle, Samantha took aim and connected with the red dot of a drone just as it swerved to get them in its sights.

KA-BOOM!

It exploded, taking down two next to it.

"That's why the hell we keep you around," Dan whooped in victory. "Thanks for the reminder."

He ducked around the corner and let out a series of shots, then flung himself back and out of the way of more fire.

"Dammit, Dan!" Ashley's voice sounded through Dan's earpiece and from the other roof at the same time, reminding Samantha that she hadn't put her own earpiece back in yet.

She did so just in time to nearly go deaf as Ashley shouted, "Get off that roof!"

"She's right," Samantha said. "Go!"

He shook his head and was about to argue, when his eyes went wide and he aimed his blaster over Samantha's shoulder. She felt the vibration through his arm as it came to rest against her, and then he was pulling her toward the stairs.

"You go, I'll hold them off."

"No, Dan—" She was cut off by an intense whirring as five drones appeared behind him, the red circles at their noses already lit, ready to fire.

Without time to think, without the slightest bit of hesitation, Samantha aimed in, focused on the farthest drone. She took a deep breath and squeezed the trigger as an intense warmth flooded through her muscles. But her weapon never went off. Instead she sat there, staring, as the drone she had focused on shook, rattling, and everything froze in place except for the mechanized beast.

Samantha stared, amazed and confused.

Time moved again as the drone shook harder, turned red-hot, and then exploded, taking down the rest of them with it. The blast sent Samantha and Dan tumbling down the stairs, and he landed on top of her with an "Oompth" as her head smacked the floor.

At first she saw stars, blue stars, then realized they were his eyes, inches from her. Close enough to kiss her. She cocked her head, and as out of place as the thought was... she hoped he would.

But no, he was shouting something, his lips moving. And then he had her, pulling her up.

"Are you okay?" The words came like a distant whisper, accompanied by a dull ringing that grew louder and then suddenly popped, allowing his voice to come in clear this time. "Sam, are you with me?"

She nodded, eyes wide. *Holy cajoles,* she thought.

What had happened? Had she had something to do with that?

"Must've been a malfunction," Dan said, wrapping an arm around her and leading her down the stairs as fast as they could go. He holstered his blaster and pressed his earpiece back in. "Ashley, you up there? We're making our way back."

"Copy that," Ashley said through their earpieces, her voice shaky. "They're all down... I don't know what the hell happened, but they're all down."

"Malfunction," Dan repeated, but for the slightest second his eyes flittered over to Samantha. There was awe there. Terror-filled awe, but definitely awe.

He had seen her do it!

With a smile at the fact that she no longer doubted herself, and that he had looked at her like that, she said into her earpiece, "Gunny, you out there?"

"Yeah, girl," Gunny's raspy voice replied. "What you got for me?"

"We're coming out, me and Danny boy. Get everyone in place, we're taking over this mech."

"Cheer-E-Os!" Gunny called back in his gung-ho way.

"Just... get everyone ready, you corny S.O.B.," Dan said into his earpiece, then paused at the second-to-last stairwell down, hands on Samantha's shoulders as he stared into her eyes.

"Um...?"

"Checking for a concussion," he said, then nodded and released her. "You ready for this?"

She nodded back.

"And whatever that was... up there. Think you can do it again, if needed?"

This time she grinned with a more enthusiastic nod.

"I've got some questions for you when this is all done," he said. "Maybe an apology too, for ever doubting you. I'd say a drink, if you're old enough?"

"We'll figure something out." The words slipped out, and she blushed at the sound of them.

His eyes went wide, apparently seeing right through her. She wanted to meld into the wall behind her, just become part of it and sink out of existence.

But then his smile returned and he shook his head with a chuckle. "Just... keep those bastards off of me if they return, got it?"

She nodded, wanting to thank him for ignoring her accidental flirtation.

With a wave of his hand, he was off, and she was forced back to thoughts on their present situation instead of teenage swooning. Probably for the best, she told herself. Right now she needed to stay focused.

They emerged from the dim stairwell into the blinding light of day. A vibration rumbled through the ground, and then another, quicker and quicker.

"Mech incoming!" Gunny shouted over the earpieces.

Dan took off at a sprint, only pausing long enough to turn back and say, "Hurry your ass!"

"Sam," Gunny said, "get in position six!"

"And follow your damn orders this time," Ashley chimed in.

"On it!" Samantha replied, breaking off from Dan to turn left past an old thrift store recently turned to rubble. She moved along the side streets of what had once been Cleveland. The smell of smoke and gunpowder hung in the chilly air, and sometimes the team would joke that it sure was cold for hell.

She darted past Gunny, gave a nod, and found her spot at an improvised bunker at the edge of their block where she could see the incoming mech.

Holy balls, she thought as she set the thing in her sights. It was huge, bounding forward with each step and given an extra boost from thrusters at its back. While most would think of mechs as smooth or angled like a tank, this one was clearly meant to be part kill-machine, part intimidation. Its back was ridged to give it an alien look, its face glowing red. Spikes rose from its arms above the cannon on one side and the blaster on the other.

THUD. THUD. THUD.

"Almost on us!" she shouted.

"I'm in place," Dan's smooth voice came back. "You tell me when."

She waited, feeling each heartbeat send her blood coursing through her skull. A warm tingling went through her, and she wondered if it was an aftereffect of whatever she had done on the rooftop, or simply a rush from the thrill of the moment.

"NOW!" she shouted, and everything moved into double time. She was up, firing at the mech's feet, and then retreating into the nearby building to distract it.

BOOM!

Its cannon took out a twelve-foot radius of the area where she had just been standing. Lucky for her, she moved fast. A rattling sounded as its shoulder gun readied, but she was hurrying past the next building already, preparing to loop back around.

More shots sounded, and she knew Ashley had taken her spot on the roof. More explosions, followed by shouting in the earpiece, and then Samantha was in her second position.

Where was that son of a bitch?

She glanced around, seeing only rubble and smoke. Beyond all that, more smoke rose in the distance— black, thick. Was that… it was!

"Gunny, we got smoke coming from the direction of home base!" she shouted into her earpiece.

"Dammit, Sam!" he replied. "Stay focused."

"But Gunny—"

"I KNOW! Ain't nothing we can do about it right now but keep to the mission. We get this mech, we score a point against the Syndicate. Right now, we need a damn point."

If the Syndicate is really our ultimate enemy, Sam

thought, remembering her visions of the end of the world. Remembering what the man, or alien, whatever he was, had shown her. Hadrian… that was his name.

And if her power was real, then so was he.

The validation hit her like a punch to the throat, and for a moment she couldn't breathe. All her memories came flooding back to her.

Then, she saw him.

A quick glimpse—at first a tail of smoke, then a man in a robe. He was gone when she looked again, but it was enough to rattle her.

If he was back, why? Why now?

"Sam, you got eyes on the mech?" Dan asked.

She spun, searching, and then… *THUD. THUD. THUD.* It appeared around the corner, its massive metal spikes of blue and red facing her.

"It's got its back to me, facing your way," she hissed.

"I'm going for it," Dan replied.

"It's too risky!"

"Risk?" Dan chuckled, though it was a nervous one. "Risk is what we're doing, Sam. We're out here risking our lives for everyone back there, and I mean to see it through."

Sure, Samantha thought as she glanced back at the smoke coming from the direction of their base. If anyone was back there to keep alive anymore.

"AHHH!" Dan shouted, and then he appeared, leaping from a building and going straight for the mech. While she and others opened fire—away from the mech so as not to hit Dan—the mech turned, ready to engage, and Dan did his magic.

"The plate's off," he said. "Connecting wires."

"We've got more drones incoming!" Ashley shouted, and Gunny cursed.

"Give me thirty seconds!" Dan hissed.

More gunfire, the sound of the mech's cannon, and then an explosion.

"I'm hit!" Gunny said. "Holy Eggo-Waffle balls that hurts!"

"Stay put," Ashley said, "I'm coming for you!"

"Dammit, Ash," Gunny replied. "Stay where the hell you are! Dan needs you!"

"I can get to you," Sam said, turning to see where she had last seen Gunny. "How's that mech looking, Dan?"

"Got the wires, just—"

"Don't you dare, Sam!" Gunny shouted. "Everyone stay put. Just… a little… blood. I'll…"

Silence followed. Or, as much silence as could while buildings exploded from a mech going berserk and three LRR fighters shooting to distract it.

"Gunny's… down… HE'S DOWN!"

"DAMMIT!" Ash screamed.

After a moment, Dan's voice came through again. "And… we got the mech."

It was a moment of horrible internal conflict. Gunny had been important to the cause, and yet, this had been something they'd been working toward.

Something they knew had the possibility to turn around the fate of the Resistance.

Still, no amount of success could make up for the pain tearing through Sam's chest over the loss of Gunny. It was almost unbearable, but it wasn't the first time they'd lost someone, and wouldn't be the last. If they let this stall them, then that meant they would have let it beat them.

"Get that mech moving, Dan," Samantha said over the comms. "We've gotta go."

"For the love of—" Ashley started, but Dan cut her off.

"She's right. Gunny would've wanted it."

Silence.

Whirring again. LOUD WHIRRING. Samantha spun to see a pack of drones coming her way, rising up and taking aim.

"We've got company!" she screamed, backpedaling.

They aimed in, the lights of their targeting systems creating red lines in her eyes. Her mind was telling her to reach for the gun and shoot, or run. Anything but sit there like a target.

Bullets started flying, and she could see them in slow motion, emerging from the barrels. It was as if time had slowed and now... stopped.

A flash of red and black, an arm around her torso, another under her legs, and she was at the next building over as time reset and the drones pulverized the empty spot where she had been a split-second before.

Her vision cleared, and she saw her rescuer.

Hadrian.

His face was fluid, changing before her eyes. It settled on an image he knew she would find pleasing, if not slightly disturbing. Especially since she still wasn't totally convinced her memories of him were real.

A man in his forties, salt-and-pepper hair with a bit of stubble, and the same smile as her mom. It was what she sometimes imagined her dad might look like, even though she had no way of knowing. She had never met the douchebag Marine who impregnated her mom and then took off.

The drones whirred, confused. Then they zipped away, sensing something around the corner.

"We have to go back for them!" Sam shouted, struggling to break free from Hadrian. "They already got Gunny! We can't just…"

She trailed off as gunfire sounded nearby, followed by explosions and then more gunfire and shouting.

"Dammit." She pushed Hadrian away and fell to the rooftop. Another wave of drones appeared, followed by a second loud stomping toward them.

"This is the time," Hadrian said, holding out a hand for her to take. "This is your time."

"What the hell are you talking about?" She pulled her rifle around, aiming in on the drones and firing. Now they were on to her, but at least she'd kept them away from the shit-storm that was happening down below.

Hadrian closed his eyes and held out a hand. A pulse of energy like a shockwave flew out from him and hit the closest drone, causing it to start vibrating. The other drones zipped around it as the mech came within feet, then the vibrations stopped. All sound seemed to cease, and then—

KA-BOOM!

All of the drones were blasted by the explosion, tearing them to pieces as the mech below was knocked onto its back, its control box shattered and its shields down.

"This is bigger than them, Sam," Hadrian said, and this time he didn't wait for her to take his hand. He grabbed her, picking her up, and turned from the battle.

"Nothing's bigger than them!"

He sighed, looking at her and then at the devastation below, and said, "I'll show you. They will be fine."

In a flash, they were on a completely different rooftop. Samantha saw the first mech go running by, glide forward with its thrusters, and strafe across an opening between buildings as it unleashed with a blaster that took out the last two drones.

She couldn't believe Dan had really done it. With a yelp of excitement, she ran to the edge of the roof, looking for them. She spotted him with his controls on the opposite side of the street, within the skeleton of a building.

He moved his head as if about to look up, and her hand raised in return. But then something caused him to look behind him instead. A moment later, Ashley was there, jumping into his arms, laughing. And then… they were kissing.

It hit Samantha like a lead pipe. She couldn't breathe. Her muscles tensed and her vision blurred, and then the window beside Ashley and Dan started to vibrate. They both turned and looked up, but Hadrian yanked Samantha away.

"This is precisely why you must come with me," he said. He moved a hand out in front of him and a gateway opened. "You have the power, now you must learn to control it."

"That wasn't me. I can't—"

"Yes, it was, and you can. One more minute, and those people you care so much about would've been full of shards of glass, thanks to your inability to control what I have taught you." He smiled, though the smile looked unnatural on his face. "Now, it's time you reached the next level."

"But the Resistance, they need me."

"Sam, look at me." He held her shoulders, staring into her eyes. "You have been fighting for Earth, but not in the way you think. What I'm offering is for you to be part of an elite team, one of several chosen to go up against the real enemy here. An enemy I've hinted at before, but only now will you begin to truly comprehend."

She felt like she had tasted a cake and loved it, then had the whole thing shoved into her face. How the hell was she supposed to process all of this?

Hadrian added, "What you'll be fighting for from now on isn't just Earth. It's much more. Sam, you'll be fighting for the fate of the universe."

How does one argue that? Samantha was here for the fight, and if there was an opportunity to take it to the next level, she was ready. Or at least, she couldn't say no. She only wished she had been told earlier.

Turning to the flowing light of the jump point, she steeled any remaining doubts, pushed them deep down, and then burned the hell out of them with her passion and determination. No more room for doubts. No more room for failure.

She stepped into the gate, ready to save the universe.

Everything went black, then lights flashed around her and she lost consciousness.

Visions returned of massive spider mechs and aliens so vile she wanted to turn and cry at the sight of them. An assault on Earth opened before her like a veil being lifted to reveal the universe, all of it in chaos.

And then she was in a bed, a cold sweat on her brow. She sat up, looking around, confused. Her head ached and her stomach clenched and unclenched repeatedly. How long had the travel taken? Where was she, and when was the last time she had eaten?

Then she noticed the man at the end of the room, and he noticed her. No, not a man, but man-like. Humanoid, but with translucent skin and eyes that looked like they were literally balls of fire.

He cocked his head, said something muted and indistinct, and then walked toward her.

Samantha's heart fluttered, her mouth went dry, and then... she fell back to the bed, once again unconscious.

AUTHOR NOTES

Jonathan Yanez

Well, well, well look who decided to come back for more. And I'm so glad that you did! Saying a simple thank you doesn't seem like enough. You are my family. Not just because you read my books or because you're reading the author note at the end of book three but because you and I are the same.

We both love stories and our imaginations know no bounds. We're from the same tribe, the same pack, the very same clan. You're my people.

Okay, that was starting to get a little mushy so back to sharing with you what's been going on in my neck of the woods. War Wolves has done better than any of my previous books and I have you to thank for that. The way you have embraced Riot and her crew has far exceeded even my wildest expectations and that's saying something because you've seen my imagination and it's pretty out there.

The sales numbers for War Wolves have come in and the numbers don't even look real. I think I'm still kind of processing the success of the series. I've refused to let my day to day routine change. Everyday I stay home with my daughter and we play and color and I write while she naps or at night I'm up late after she lays her tiny head to rest.

I promise not to let the success of War Wolves go to my head. My reward to myself once the money comes in is a new pair of gym shorts I needed since one of the drawstrings on my other pair of shorts mysteriously gut sucked into that little hole it comes out of in the waistline.

You know what I'm talking about right? It happens to a

lot of hoodies that have drawstrings too. One day out of the wash that lace you pull has for some reason receded into the hole all on its own.

Never mind, this conversation is all to say that I'm being smart with my success. I'm hard at work on the next project and plan on using the money that's coming in wisely to help support my wife and daughter.

I feel like I owe so many of you another thank you for leaving reviews on both Bring the Thunder and Click Click Boom. I have tough skin from so many years in sales but for some reason there was a review left the other day on Bring the Thunder that really bothered me. I think it was because the review kept using my first name like he knew me. That's what probably what made the attack feel so personal.

After reading that rough review I was trying to figure out why I was letting his words bother me so much. I was trying to fend off the voices in my head that demanded I spend more and more time thinking about it when you freaking awesome wolves came to the rescue and didn't even know it!

Within hours of that demeaning review I received two more stellar reviews on Bring the Thunder and another on Click Click Boom. Immediately that reaffirmed confidence on who I write for. I wrote for brothers and sisters like you, not some two bit, yahoo who I don't know from Adam.

So thank you again wolves. If you keep on reading and enjoying the stories coming out of my twisted imagination I promise I'll keep writing them.

What's ahead for the future? Well I'm so glad you decided to ask. Since I wrapped production on book three in the War Wolves series I've been hard at work on another project that will be dropping in a few months. Think Old Man Logan meets We Were Soldiers and you're close. It's a single story set in another pair of well known authors' universe.

In January I also get the rights back from a trilogy of stories under a publisher I used when I was first starting off. I plan to rebrand the series with new covers and blurbs and add more content to the books.

After that I have plans to start my own sci-fan (science fantasy) universe. I'm really excited to break ground on that series. If you're not part of my pack on Facebook I want to send you a personal invitation <CLICK HERE> or if you'd rather be notified by email <CLICK HERE> and join the pack's newsletter so we can stay in touch.

I hope you decide to keep in contact. I'm off to write some more words before my daughter wakes up from her nap. You are the very best. You promise not to change and I'll do the same.

See you on the other side,

Jonathan

Justin Sloan

Three books are now out in the series, and at the time of writing we have found out who our narrator will be (she sounds AMAZING). Podium is doing a great job with the audiobooks in the Seppukarian Universe, this one included. Why is a cool company like Podium excited about all of this? Because of readers like you.

The main feedback I have heard from readers is that these books are fun. Know what? That's exactly the word Jonathan kept using when describing what he was trying to accomplish here—fun. It's the word I've heard so many readers of my other series say is the reason they keep coming back, and so we're going to keep on focusing on making FUN stories, as long as you keep reading.

Having fun while reading is why we keep at it, right? For a lot of us, anyway, it's about escaping whatever else is going on, whether it's depression, boredom, stress, whatever. And in many ways these stories work as a way of making us forget these problems, or even giving us courage that we can rise up and defeat whatever's in our way.

Got some crappy boss you can't stand anymore? Well, don't be like Riot and use weapons to solve this problem, but be like her in that you won't give up, you won't sit around and wallow in self-pity. Would she sit around at the water cooler and complain? Hell no! In that situation, I have no idea what she would do, lol, but I imagine she would kick butt on her next project so she gets the recognition she deserves, or maybe go out there and start networking like crazy so that when the right job opportunity arrives, she's ready.

Of course, some problems are not beaten, right? Cancer, for example. We can't just punch it in the face and conquer it, as much as we'd all love to. But we can find fellowship, we can change our mindset to not let it defeat us mentally. It's tough, and I think fiction like this helps us through these kind of things. Maybe I'm giving too much credit to books and you think I sound like an idiot, right? That's fine. But I know this is the case for me and MANY of my readers who write quite often describing exactly this situation. When we receive those notes, it's incredibly touching. I can't begin to tell you how many times I've gotten teary eyed and, when my wife asked me what's wrong, I've told her I was reading another email from a reader. You all give us the inspiration and courage to keep putting ourselves out there, and we thank you for it form the bottom of our hearts.

Okay, enough sappy stuff. What's next? We have more amazing books coming in the Seppukarian Universe, so stay tuned! And if you liked these, you might like my scifi books that I'm doing in the Kurtherian Gambit universe—VALERIE'S ELITES. I also have some sweet solo works coming in 2018, so be ready!

If you liked the books, please leave reviews, follow us on Amazon so you don't miss new releases, and keep in touch. Thank you again!

Justin